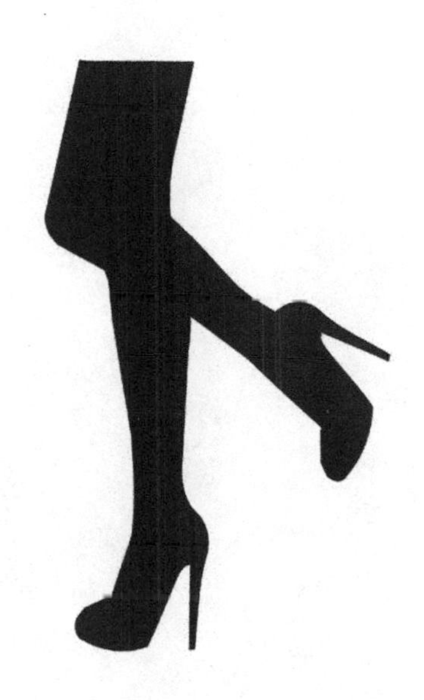

Waiting for Sophia

at Shutters on the Beach

A Novel by

Aris Janigian

REGENT PRESS
Berkeley, California

[Hardback]
ISBN 13: 978-1-58790-509-4
ISBN 10: 1-58790-509-4

[Paperback]
ISBN 13: 978-1-58790-510-0
ISBN 10: 1-58790-510-8

Library of Congress Control Number: 2019942798

Manufactured in the U.S.A.
REGENT PRESS
Berkeley, California
www.regentpress.net

Puritanism is a backlash against decadence, but, in almost every instance, it is also its final phase and refinement.

— *from* Decadence and Farce from Warhol to Koons

One night, while he was praying, he heard a voice cry, "Ha! Abu'l-Hasan! Dost thou wish Me to tell the people what I know of thee, that they may stone thee to death?" "O Lord God," he replied, "dost Thou wish me to tell the people what I know of Thy mercy and what I perceive of Thy grace, that none of them may ever again bow to Thee in prayer?" The voice answered, "Keep thy secret, and I will keep Mine."

— *from* Reynold A. Nicholson, The Mystics of Islam

For all my amazing friends,
who've given me shelter from the storm, and
who've pushed me into it.

I was seated in the glamorous Living Room at Shutters on the Beach, having ordered my first martini from the Abercrombie and Fitch–handsome waiter, who introduced himself as Zeke, when Sophia texted to apologize that she was, true to form, running late. Naturally, a woman as beautiful as Sophia is instantly forgiven for such a peccadillo, but I was also happy for the extra time to leisurely reflect on our most uncommon friendship and perhaps confect ever more extravagant romantic fantasies about her.

One of a professor's perennial perks used to be getting to seduce or gladly accept the advances of your prettiest, and in Sophia's case, most intelligent students, but now the environment was so hostile to any carnal encounter not sanctioned by the new priestesses, along with more than a few prissy priests, one was forced to consider whether even shagging a thirty-three-year-old alum was taboo, or rather, near-alum, as Sophia had disappeared from school, leaving her dissertation—*Decadence and Farce from Warhol to Koons*—unfinished, the very reason she innocently reached out to me for this rendezvous, to help her decide whether to push through or drop out of the program and remain a so-called adjunct for the balance of her academic life.

I say "innocently," but there was hardly anything this woman wasn't thoroughly briefed on, if not wonderfully corrupted in. Her sheer worldliness and ingenuity at surviving in any environment had provided safe sailing while a student, but I'd always felt the perilous speed at which her brain turned would be her eventual undoing, even if she graduated and a thousand tenure tracks suddenly lined up for the taking. But where was my drink? Ah, there Zeke was chatting it up with a forty-something waitress, likely comparing depressing notes on their latest audition results.

What a disaster these actors inflict upon their tender persons, ricocheting from here to there for casting calls and auditions and classes at Strasberg and Adler, only to end up five or so years into it chucked aside like road kill by the dream they had chased. Los Angeles is like some amber palace that from a distance mystically glows but get up close and you'll discover millions of insects stuck in the sap. Precisely like the academy, and these adjuncts, I thought, who daily endure defilements that would cause de Sade to cringe. We ladle beans and grits onto their glum plastic plates while just outside the cafeteria ribbon cuttings in celebration of one glittering administrative palace after another proceed with spectacular regularity. It's gotten to the point that we, the tenured class, are required almost by job description to forsake our belief in parity and civility and exhibit the most miserable mock collegiality toward these lumpen, to the extent that I actually wince when I see them sitting in their pint-sized offices hoping to be taken seriously by anyone other than the student who is dimly aware of how powerless this person in power is, the one grading papers for hours on end while stripped of the most elementary safeguards that dignified work from the days of Carnegie. We endlessly worry that the transgendered have a comfortable place to pee while utterly oblivious to the drones dropping their cluster bombs on the janitors and gardeners and cooks and dishwashers, all the subhumans whose vocal cords need severing to make this place sing! If all that weren't enough, witness how predictably the cornered corner each other, how one finds no sense of solidarity among these adjuncts, but rather the most craven and pathetic backbiting and infighting over classes and seniority, which amounts to little more than who gets to shit first in the field hand's outhouse.

That said, Sophia was not, as was too often sadly the case these days, living out of a car on her instant-ramen-scale salary, because she always tended to her own needs meticulously. Perhaps she had cohabitated with the real estate mogul she met soon after leaving school long enough he'd ponied up a small portion of his vast equity in a palimony settlement, as I'd discovered she was now luxuriating in her own three-bedroom condo in Brentwood. I could see her cudgeling the real estate mogul with her sizeable beauty and diabolic intellect until he was cut to a stump, just as she'd cut to a stump all these sexually willowy peers of hers who'd go for their rosaries whenever she so much as entered a room. Ah, Sophia. Don't stutter, or, god forbid, stare at her! But one must, for the flawless symmetry of every one-in-a-trillion-chance feature of which this marvel of creation is composed.

In fact, we gatekeepers of culture used to let our jaws drop at every marvel of creation, all that shook to the core and was rare—frankly bored if not contemptuous of the sweetly tempered, the level and square. Where did our quest for all that makes the human situation soar, beauty and verity, transcendence and light, get quashed? When did we settle for spinning cocoons, spaces, let's call them "safe," where we can nervously nurse the most incongruous wounds? How did "woe is me" take the place of "the truth will set you free"? Honestly, isn't it enough I am made in this world to manhandle the tempest within my own soul that I must now walk in the shoes of every retarded little twister and be left spinning around their unbridled neuroses as if upon them the entirety of the cosmos turned? Sophia might slip into Polish to describe the rattling wraiths full of complaints we've become. *Co za katastrofa.*

Ah, here it was, your first drink, on a round serving platter, which Zeke lifted from the stem and set on the table, olive facing to the side, with such studied finesse you instantly forgave him for squandering his youth for the remotest hopes of becoming a star, and, of course, making you wait.

I confess, the pressure I'd recently endured was pushing me to extremes, and, as well, to two or three drinks too many two or three hours earlier than was wise. I believed, wrongly, as it turned out, I'd retreated into my private world of literary studies successfully, sidestepping without too much headache or heartache my younger colleagues whose work I might have found ridiculous if not obscurantist but in no way hostile to me personally. Okay, perhaps I voiced an off word or two for our last hire, a lesbian/poet/activist/scholar whose research interests were whales, queers, and Honduran refugees, a trifecta of the aggrieved, but, what with her poems that included uncanny simulations of a humpback's harrowing songs, I was hardly the only one among us who had reached the breaking point. Yes, I thought I was sheltered, until the moment I was chosen by our deadbeat assistant dean to adjudicate, along with four other faculty members, a case of campus rape and found myself caught up in a protest so loud it was threatening to drown out any other sound. I had a ferocious, almost primordial impulse to slice through the clamor only to find, at the last moment, a huge hand reaching for my scabbard, a domesticating and shaming hand that, upon consideration, proved to be unmistakably that of a maternal figure hovering psychotically over a cowering boy, yes, the cake-baking femme fatale who comes each and every time in the name of learning and love. Though I ached to ask what or who was leading this absurdity's charge, the admonition "reason, calm" was all I mustered in response, and at considerable risk, as I was now made to understand that reason and calm implied a degree of detachment that was itself a conceit of the privileged.

The event in question occurred around 1:00 a.m. on a Saturday night, about two months ago, when a student of no particular distinction or attractiveness had hit on a girl at a dorm party. He was a junior doing art history, and she a fine arts major, where the cerebral side of their fling likely started, and after perhaps an hour spent discussing the relative merits of Kosuth and Richter, and blasting through four or five 16 oz. plastic cups of Sam Adams, he'd taken her by the hand up to his second-story dorm room where they clearly hoped to get something more considerable than art talk going. As they climbed the stairs she had the odd feeling he wanted something more than she might care to tender, nonetheless she proceeded quite by volition, if not per the most mundane sexual instinct, into his room and, to get cozy, studied an assortment of art hanging on the walls: a Twombly poster from the Tate he'd acquired during a semester abroad in London, what appeared to be a signed Chagall lithograph he claimed to have bought at auction but was actually an eBay deal, and a cut-paper silhouette print titled *Gone*, by far and away his favorite contemporary artist, he claimed, Kara Walker, whom the girl also revered for her electrifying use of the most elemental visual imagery to dismantle the racist tropes upon which America was horrifyingly founded. Their mutual attraction to Walker and presumably each other called for a nightcap, and he presently broke open a small-batch vodka he'd bought during a recent retreat with his parents in the meditative little town of Ojai. The vodka was smooth enough to not require a mixer, and, we discover, the two began taking bottle shots while perusing massive Abrams and Rizzoli art monographs he'd inherited from his uncle's estate the year before. All was going well until he started flipping through Modigliani, whose subjects' super-exposed necklines and blank eyes reflected, the woman said, the artist's vampiric disposition, a most diabolical misogynistic bent that could in no way be corrected by his purported artistic genius. He was an admirer of Modigliani, particularly his *Elvira Resting at a Table*, and at the risk of jeopardizing the sexual rapport budding between them, balked, contending that the artist's choice to blank his subjects' eyes was meant to create an opening into their minds, similar to Malevich's black squares where what seemed to push you away was actually a window onto infinity. "Or a blackboard announcing school is out," she enigmatically demurred. The friction didn't last long, if it didn't, in fact, generate some heat, we surmise, because she scooted to the foot of the bed and in front of a long hanging mirror shed her long stockings, pulled up her dress, spread her legs, and began fingering herself through her panties. With his back to the headrest, he now doffed his khakis, scooted up behind her and massaged her shoulders, and, careful not to break her self-spell, said, "Keep with it; it's a turn on." She did keep with it, pretty involvedly, until he became pretty near superfluous, and so, to get in on the action, he pulled her onto her back and got some kissing going, leaving his skivvies for the moment on. Off was around the bend, as presently she stood and asked him to unzip her dress, which he did, pushing it down a little forcefully, only because, he claimed, she was a little heavy and the dress was a little tight. Back in the sack, it heated up fast, so much so that the single window in the tiny 10' x 10' room must've steamed up, we infer, because at one point she peeled away to let the moment come to an even better boil and with a finger sketched a five-pointed star in a circle on the pane, because, she said, as an artist and once-upon-a-time Wiccan, she felt like it.

Back in the sack, and perhaps sensing something about her was a tad black, he kind of coxswained her onto her belly and bit her neck and pressed her wrists against the mattress, curious, clearly, to turn her on. Maybe he'd seen examples of it on the Internet, because he didn't appear to be in the least learned in any manner of S & M beyond this beginner's version. He began fingering her from the back and, as it was generally wet down there, at some point he had a go at the other hole. Uncomfortable, she pushed his hand away and said "no," after which he obliged doggie style for a while, then flipped to mish, and then cowgirl, and doggie once more, this time with a few and apparently welcome slaps to her ass. He pulled out to ease up on his gathering O, then squared up and had at it again, at which point she let out a banshee-like cry and folded into a Z and shuddered so wildly for a beat he honestly thought she'd had an epileptic fit. Having never been down that (wrong) road before, and impotent to console, he gathered her clothes and placed them at her feet, thinking she'd want back into them sooner rather than later. After a few minutes, and controlling, just barely, her breath, she jumped up and into her dress and dashed out of the room with the rest of her clothes pressed against her chest.

Drips by Eminem was booming from the room next door, so no one heard the screams, and neither did the two women seated at the end of the long hallway checking their Twitter feeds and munching on carrots initially think much of the figure staggering their way, and only when they saw tears streaming down her face did they grow concerned and ask what was up. She told them a guy down the hall had assaulted her, whereupon they rushed her into their room and called the campus police. They arrived within half an hour and took her statement, where the pushing down of her dress and pressing down of her wrists, the forced fingering and *coup de grâce* with his dick were portrayed in the most textbook molestation terms. When finished, the officers, both men, went to his room to take his statement but he'd left (to close down a party in another dorm). They took her to the campus station where she sat on her ass (without physical complaint) for an hour, the only female officer who was qualified to conduct the exam tied up with a brawl at one of the fraternities. This frustrated the victim not only because she assumed her case would be approached in a timelier manner but also because she needed to hit the john and reasoned she might accidentally contaminate the evidence if she did. The female officer, an oddly introverted woman whose physical aspect reminded me distinctly of Emily Dickinson, finally arrived and took her into the examination room, where she inspected her top to bottom and took pictures and broke out a rape kit, which involved swabbing here and there. Afterward, she was offered contact information for the counseling center and escorted back to her room. The next morning, the accused gave his side of the story, whereupon the campus police put it all together, reviewed the case in-house, decided that there wasn't enough evidence to make a felony rape case of it, and moved it along anyway to the bureaucrats charged to handle such matters. The lack of urgency and generally relaxed pace, including taking of notes and shuffling of papers, the inhumanely procedural way the campus police went about their investigation, the suggestion that she could remotely have been a willing party to the incident, raised the young woman's indignation to a pitch. So the next day she went to the city police, who likewise passed, having more straightforward rape cases to investigate, this one perhaps exceptional to the point of sui generis.

Now confident that the entire system was patriarch run, in program and protocol drawn up by men to preserve their dominance over women, to the extent that even female officers were blindly inculcated into the evil realm, within three days she unleashed a letter to the assistant dean's office demanding the administration do not only a top-to-bottom review of her complaint but also the campus police's demeaning conduct in general. Not long thereafter, a lawyer's letter came crashing onto the assistant dean's ridiculous desk, sending an entire administrative wing flailing. Immediately, the deadbeat, who spent most of his time calculating how to best filet his underlings without them flinching, convened the faculty members next in line for such committee work to do a wholesale review of the school's "definition of consent," hence my involvement. And yes, I did find it ironical that a relative letch like me was at the table of deliberation. Would any day now one or another student I had made love to during my early years on campus materialize with the charge I had raped and not merely ravished her?

I looked out at the ocean, at its weird and waxing power in the shattering moonlight, and thought, for all its rumbling, whisking, and slashing sounds, let's face it, one could just as well be sitting next to a freeway. Yet somehow just knowing that it was the ocean, with its vast and deeply rooted tumult, brought consciousness to a mysterious if not romantic surrender, the way it did when you were a kid tromping through the sand with your mother who toted a picnic basket and blanket to a perfect spot not too far not too close to the shore. Ah, the squawking gulls and delicately stepping sandpipers pecking for whatever washed up in the bubbling tide and the sea sun pulsing on your skin, elemental as mother's milk. The blue knitted sweater mother now with her fingers and a small shoulder shrug slid off, revealing her freckled back and her yellow bikini straps. How she folded the sweater into a package fit for a birthday box and placed it at the blanket's edge, before taking a band from her pocket and slipping it between fingers that seemed to have eyes for how nimbly they tied back her hair, all so that her wide-brimmed hat to guard her face from the sun had a neat place to sit. What finesse mothers possessed, how this goes here and that goes there, the most delicate rituals to keep danger at bay were at their fingertips: Where did she learn these rituals? In the mysterious world of girls is where. As I absently built castles in the sand, I wondered how different was that world from the brutish and rudimentary one I was forced to join. Was there a way to grow into manhood and at the same time stay seated within the feminine realm? She now opened a book and lay down on her side to read, with her breasts on fulsome display, her legs extending exquisitely from her shortest of white shorts. I see the way she comes up from her book when I get bored and run toward the waves, the way she keeps watch as the tide makes my feet disappear, and the way she puts her reading aside and lets the rest of the world go about its business as she goes about hers, me.

A waiter other than my own stepped up to my table with a smile. "Professor, I had Shakespeare with you eight or so years ago." "You look familiar, but . . ." I said, putting out my hand and leaving the reverie of my mother. "Jonathan Graham." "Yes," I said, "how are you?" "I wanted to stop, to tell you how much that class meant to me, how much I looked forward to it. I remember that beautiful classroom we had on College Avenue. A great wood-paneled room with double-hung windows and a big mahogany table we used to sit around, about twelve of us." I was impressed he remembered the room where I regularly taught Shakespeare, as beautiful as he remembered. "I was going law postgrad, but did an MFA in writing instead," he said. "Really. A screenwriter?" Such were a ghastly number of writers in this city. "In a roundabout way," he said. "These days some people are writing novels first and then adapting them into screenplays." "Roundabout indeed. A novel. Well, it's quite a river to cross. I wish you the best." "I'm about finished with a first draft." "And how would you describe the book?" It featured an orphaned, homeless person, half-black and half-white, searching for his identity, a kind of metaphor for the ambiguity of this and the ontology of that, with a plot so Escheresque, so far as I could determine from his brief description, it would require a companion book, and one nobody would want to read, to understand. I thought, please, spare me, it will never work; when you need a book to explain your book, either you are in Faulkner's league, or you aren't—there is no merciful in-between. "Sounds quite interesting," I said, perhaps not as convincingly as I'd hoped. "Thanks," he said, "have a good evening." I was always of the mind writers should avoid other writers, egotists one and all, except for a drink or verbal brawl, and instead scour the streets alone to gather their precious and scabrous material; to spend two or more years in a classroom in the prime of your sniffing and pawing life seemed an outrage to the profession, but entirely in keeping with the nauseating timidity of this so-called millennial generation and its almost lethal sponginess.

Ah, you could still rely on a martini, its lovely cold crispness, the small green olive and its small swirling juices—how many just such martinis had provided a lubricant for any number of seductions. Odds were Sophia would know perfectly well that I had reserved this table at this beautiful bar overlooking one of our most beautiful beaches with the intent to proposition her, after, naturally, offering earnest guidance regarding the course her future should take. I thanked my lucky stars we hadn't met as students on any number of college campuses today, as we'd be forced to humiliate ourselves with some consent form before the seduction could commence, in which case all the exquisite theatrics of seduction would be reduced to a farce. Fear of seduction was everywhere in the air these days, as was the fear of giving oneself over to a poem or novel, I thought. The same way people were afraid of being seduced by the shattering charms of a novel so were people afraid of being seduced by the shattering charms of a lover. Above and beyond anything else, so the current regime exhorts, one must resist being seduced because the moment one is seduced one has conceded power to the seducer. They imagine there is nothing more debasing and horrifying when, in fact, there is nothing more exhilarating and even edifying than losing one's farcical and imagined freedom, especially to one whose diabolical powers one barely fathoms. The entire enterprise of great writing is to take you to a place you're afraid to go to and disarticulate you head to hoof, leaving you hanging like a happy carcass there for the human truth to ravish. Yes, it is true, I suppose, certain dangers attend this surrender, but we must also admit it is one of the most well-trodden paths leading to the most scintillating discoveries. What grim forfeitures of all that we've worked to perfect over thousands of years are now required of us in this new dispensation.

I looked up from these thoughts, took a quaff of my martini, and focused in on a couple sitting across from me, the girl, ballerina slim, light freckles and icicle-white skin with softest hint of pink, so nearly ethereal she might've been a vestal virgin there as a kind of sacrifice for the mid-fifties rocker slouched next to her on the couch whose fried black hair she presently and rather tenderly ran her beautiful bony fingers through, turning my consideration to a similarly supple strawberry from a Christian college in the Midwest who used to run her fingers through my own hair when once upon a time I had enough to satisfy a Samson. The waitress set a bowl of massive shrimp in front of them and before she could put the napkin down the rocker reached for one and dipped it into a red horseradish sauce and laid it on his tongue in so disgusting a manner that a giant lizard came to mind. His girl sipped her fancy sparkling water and watched him, as might a mother slightly concerned he'd fail to chew all the way through and choke. From the looks of his stunning hand and arm tattoos (on his weirdly depilated skin) and massive gem-studded watch, he was obviously rich if not famous enough to forego decorum as he now asked, so loudly the bartender twenty yards away must've been forced to consider, "Whethah Rohd'll aven foockin' shoo oop." Delicately, the girl scooted out of the booth and headed for the bathroom for a touching up, probably, as she'd a small and stylish makeup bag in hand. I watched him watch her go, and once she was out of sight, he pulled his hair back with his fingers and then smoothened the wrinkles from his eyes, sighing right into the vacuum her beautiful self left behind. There it was: the inner boy, what rises invariably as the sun in these types once the fandom has faded. Yes, beneath all his sartorial bravado and baroque skin quivered a faltering soul hauntingly aware of life in retreat, the creeping consciousness that the sum of his excesses and age per se had left him a crumbling simulacrum of the person much less persona he once was; that his manic dancing and sizzling lyrics and fans all swooning in holocaust-size amphitheaters had fizzled out only to leave him strumming an acoustic guitar in the cattle car of his drug-stunned brain, with, admittedly, that most covetable beauty there for balm.

Ah, the sadness of our sex, the sheer, let's here admit, preposterousness of it, starting with the moment when, from the depths of some antediluvian dream, the milky concoction first spurts, throwing into question the integrity of our heretofore single-purposed dicks. Where did this disgusting muck spawn and why is our flesh suddenly quickened for all things sensuous, including certain animals, like a sweating horse or wet and panting dog, not to mention the girl whom you were formerly repulsed by, that buxom animal who now possesses the magnetism of a neutron star, restructuring your foursquare brain into an intoxicating maze that you want to draw her into and close the only exit on. What a frightening mess night after night we make of our underwear, pajamas, and sheets, and how surreptitiously we flush the tissues at the flush of every dawn, before mom finds out, because we intuitively know that this will throw her tidy tiny kingdom into a maelstrom. All the while our fathers want nothing more than to avoid speaking of these early perturbations they'd spent years calming or escaping from by way of a thousand subtle and not-so-subtle machinations. See how this most uninvited and exhilarating *raison d'être* turns everything else into gobbledygook, especially teachers with their ream after ream of facts and concepts, a withered and odorless universe so brutally removed from our human appetites they seem generated for the sole purpose of starving us into submission. Are these adults as oblivious as they seem to the battle of the bulge raging down there, where the reality of the animal-human situation in all its obstinate glory blooms? Where all the subterfuge begins. Yes, underground we now must go, like gophers hiding from some hell-bent rancher whose regular remedy is dynamite, all this tunneling dead-ending into frustration and anger, booze and brawls, and mind-bending speeds. Some of us make a foxhole and shut a flimsy lid over our heads holding fast to the faith that somewhere down the line our bookish focus will win the orgiastic day and also for the time being ward off the succubi plaguing us from every quarter. Who will teach you to turn your weed into a flower to attract that most necessary bee?

Inch by inch, we listen and learn to the dictate that we must do it here and not there, in accord with this thesis and not that, until we've civilized our dicks to the point they are safe and useful tools in other hands besides our gummy own. Ah, what joy, within sight is our hard-earned prize, the drink of our lives, our wives, on endless tap, and for a while our cup floweth over indeed, until the seed, so tertiary to our need, find its mark, and that woman who'd been all the seductress is suddenly full of child and empty of desire.

One child, then two, and maybe more come, and so long as they do, so do you, until that branch in the genealogical tree dead-ends, and the humiliation you must face for your mostly fruitless hungering re-begins, because, let's make it plain, your function is complete if not your very sexual person obsolete. Tsk, tsk: Listen up, Richard, aka, dick: An endless host of more civilized concerns attends the family drama you have set in motion, forcing you back into that bunker, where you must now fund a thousand different proxy wars to gain a foot of ground, from once a week to once a month to a winning draw so improbable you might as well have a go at the state lottery. Ah, finally, after twenty years, you've been pulled off that arthritis-making UPS route and given your own nicely secluded cubicle where you can track deliveries and play with your pitiable self in privacy. The guy in logistics has shown you a sure-fire means of pole vaulting over the firewall but then out of nowhere a warning flashes across the screen and Human Resources is calling you in. How will you explain fuckorfired.com to that Latina gal shaped like a walnut whose husband ditched her for the sixteen-year-old babysitter, who also just so happened to be the niece she smuggled in from Mexico to help raise her five kids. At least you still have that Asian Massage Parlor on the most miserable side of town. All is going so-so with Ce-Ce there, one deplorable rung above self-help, actually, until one afternoon vice raids the place and she of "nospeekee ingrish," who a minute before made an "O" of her hand and pumped it like a bartender mixing a ($40) cocktail, is read her rights and escorted into a paddy wagon. As for your spongy bum sitting on the curb: A citation for solicitation suffices, a misdemeanor the cop almost ruefully tells you, but what apocalyptic consequences await you when your kids and wife find out, not to mention the entire community when your mug gets posted on what they call the "wall of shame," courtesy of the sheriff's department website. The sins the rich get away with: Three "G" a month could've secured for you a perfectly lawful rendezvous with a sweet-smelling sugar baby in a cozy apartment rather than a Rub-and-Tug in a converted closet reeking of Chinese Five Spice, but, as it was, you had to sneak cashbacks at the supermarket so your significant other didn't notice a sudden drain on your barely-enough-as-it-was funds. You've been spending OUR money on hand jobs? she sobs. Maybe you should have taken the time to focus on your now dishonored wife, her needs, for this, that, and every other unfathomable thing. Even if, as you claim, she has about as much enthusiasm for your schlong as she does clearing lint from the dryer, did you really try? Consider counseling, a place to sideline your adolescence for an hour a week and square up on the psychic blocks that have come between you two, including your own calamitous childhood, an alcoholic father and bipolar mother who cruelly took away your beloved picture books to punish you because at age five you were still wetting your sheets? Look inside to see how your boyish cry for satisfaction has upended fifteen years of trust and goodwill, and why, anyway, should you want it anymore anyhow? Haven't you gotten your stupid fill? Isn't it pathologically bizarre how your dick still salutes like a cub scout for whatever random ass that waves? Why should the fact I am an inch shorter and weigh twice what I did when you first wooed me matter? Haven't I toiled to hold this family together, sacrificed the better part of my life to make you and these kids happy, dealt with your mood swings, and buoyed you up when you made all those stupid business moves?

All true. She had stood by you. Now what to do? Might there be some means of getting pharmacologically neutered—after all, you still need something to scratch. The deep web suggests Thailand and estrogen injections. So your tits grow to a C cup; from couch-potatoing it for twenty years, they're damn near there already. Maybe you should follow the lead of your peers who've learned to shovel every manner of outlandishness into the stand-in hole: travelling by camper to watch the Giants at spring training in Tucson; feasting on wild boar and turkey you yourself shot! Spending seven hours a day on that toy train set up (in the spare bedroom where the eldest kid once slept) with flashing signal lights and plastic bridges and benches where lovers hold hands watching the train romantically pass with its occasional hoot and discharge of the most ironic puffs of smoke. Watch it go round and round like your thoughts, your life, your dreams. But look, the track splits, and you're chugging through a tunnel that leads to a cliff that drops cartoonishly into an abyss where your cracked ass can sit to reflect upon what all that heroism and self-sacrifice, and, yes, those sins have brought you. Where for the balance of your days you ponder the vast farce perpetuated upon you by who the fuck knows, so big is the thing, the system, the machine you've been a grinding part of.

Enough. I finished the balance of my martini in one gulp and put a hand up for Zeke, who'd disappeared as artfully as he'd placed the martini down earlier. Sophia agreed to meet at 9:00 p.m., but, as I've already mentioned, she was notoriously late, often showing up to class (always apologetically) well into a discussion and on a good number of occasions not showing up at all (usually alerting me in advance). Delinquencies out of necessity, I'd later learn. She'd taken four of my classes, all audited, and because she was in Art History, whereas I taught English with a concentration on Chaucer and Shakespeare and other Elizabethan literature, I was surprised she approached me to chair her committee. "Shouldn't you be writing under someone in your own area of study," I told more than asked her, "because, let's face it, your chances of getting a good position after graduation are a heck of a lot better if you do. It's like having children; your students are your intellectual progeny." "All true, but I still feel you are the only professor who could possibly chair my committee, so the choice is already made, if not positively fated," was her unexpected retort, whereupon I sensed something not just brilliant and original but definitely off-kilter about her, which, at the same time, was wildly seductive and too late by many years to fix. "What are you thinking of writing on?" I asked. "Decadence and farce," was her answer. In terms of farce, the reason for her choice of me now came into some kind of focus. "But farce, not in the sense we know it and explore it in literature," she explained, "not as a genre of writing, but as a critical tool we might use to pry open the American reality." (And yes, I did inwardly scoff at the lofty ambition of her dissertation. American reality? Really?)

I told her I'd talk to a couple of the professors in her department about it, but I made no promises. She was, they reported, in their classes as provocative a thinker as she was in mine, except almost since the day she entered the program she pursued a most unadvisable course, auditing a dozen or more classes outside of the department (like mine), and I shouldn't expect her to check in at any regular intervals, as she was prone to disappear for weeks on end. This explained why it had taken her four years instead of two to finish her coursework; all told, this would have gotten anyone less bright booted squarely out of the program. "We've had to rewrite the rules for her, and even then," one professor told me, "she's pushed her luck too far for some in the program, and, frankly, isn't she doing herself, once again, a disservice, with all due respect, to reach out to you instead of someone in our department? A certain self-destructive self-confidence would describe her and may harm her long-term chances of securing a position. Beyond all that, her ideas can seem at times a bit adversarial, some would say outright offensive."

I now saw her regularly at a local coffeehouse, which she insisted was far more relaxed and productive a venue to review her thesis than was my office, but soon she insisted we meet farther and farther away from campus, at bars, and then parks, the beach, and mountain trails because "how much better to discuss these matters while hiking, no?" One spring evening she begged me to join her at 9:00 p.m. at Griffith Park, only to arrive forty-five minutes late toting a wicker basket.

"You've kept me waiting. I have better things to do, and though the basket is swell, I didn't come for a picnic."

"I love the word 'swell.' Like those black-and-white Andy Griffith reruns my roommate thought I was crazy for watching when I first came to America. Everything Americans did those days seemed beautiful and innocent. 'Swell, Pa!'"

"Those things were happening only on the TV shows, I assure you."

"I don't think so," she said, "but I will not argue, Professor. Simple and innocent things are happening everywhere, all the time, but a cynical heart refuses to see them. Anyway," she said, handing the basket to me, "I thought it would be nice to graze while we stargazed."

I put the basket aside. "Stargaze?"

"Are you afraid to give the impression we're on a picnic date?"

"Now that you mention it."

"Should we submit so easily to the Stasi?"

"I think my office is going to have to suffice from here on out."

"Look, after a week of rain how clear the night sky is! I am not in love with you nor have a crush on you, Professor, but since this subject is under our nose, let's ask, who are these people to say who and how we should be attracted to one another, and under what conditions we can and cannot fall in love? The mysteries of the heart are too much for the greatest poets to unravel, much less the bureaucrats." She inhaled deeply: "The smell after such late rains. There is hardly anything left that looks like it did a thousand years ago, but here we have the chance to see back in time billions of years. It's important to get a proper measure of ourselves. Up there is our history as much as what is down here."

It sounded like a line, but I couldn't for the life of me remember who'd first said it. Carl Sagan? In any case, she opened the basket and uncorked a Fritz Haag Brauneberger Riesling, and then one by one unwrapped half a dozen or so of the most exotic cheeses she expected would pair nicely with the wine's "floral aroma and most excellent acidity."

I couldn't help but notice the prices marked in pen on the wrappers, which, in keeping with the theme of the evening as it would unfold, were astronomical.

"You see," she said, "my father was a member of Solidarity. An astronomer by training, after the wall fell he left his research behind and became a high-level diplomat." I'd always imagined a well-to-do family had paid her way through Swarthmore and set her up in that sweet Audi A6, not to mention the boutique designer dresses she sported, but now I wasn't so sure how she got her money. No Eastern European diplomat, outside a seriously corrupt one, could shower his daughter with such extravagances, and no way either could she afford it with the pittance she made teaching two classes at the local state college. "As a child, I would sit in on his discussions with his peers, and so from early on, I was taught to respect the stars and entertained by the imagination of those who studied them. The truth is, today is his birthday, and I wanted to celebrate by coming up here. I thought we could, as they say, kill two birds with one stone." Three, actually, the last being my irritation as she began to take us on the most wonderful tour of the heavens. "There, look, the usual suspects, the Big and Little Dipper, and there is Leo and the young maiden, Virgo. Too bad it is too late in the year to make out Orion, but there, the Herdsman and that most beautiful orange star at its center is called Arcturus. See?" For how hard it was for my eyes to track their geometries, "barely," I said, whereupon she directed me to what only the imagination could apprehend, farther and farther out to the far-out reaches of outer space, where from a point of pure energy millions of times smaller than an atom, in a fraction of a fraction of a second, the whole fourteen-billion-year-old cosmic business was set in motion. She explained how massive clouds of gas called stellar nurseries whipped up stars, and how these stars eventually buckled in on themselves and burst and how from the detritus everything out there was born, dust mote by dust mote, like dust balls up under your bed.

"What patience and hard work and openness to wherever the evidence leads them these scientists possess. Do you know it took us one hundred years to demonstrate that light, as Einstein predicted, does indeed bend when the light of one star passes the light of another?"

"Yes, I think I knew that."

But did I know supernovas, stars that explode, had their own dispositions: Some whip around like deranged lighthouses emitting rays so strong they reach half the length of the universe, and others are giant magnets, called, nicely, magnetars, that weigh in at 100-million-tons per thimbleful? And where our biggest stars implode, sometimes with a wink, they spawn black holes, the supermassive versions of which make galaxies like our own beautifully spiral.

"At the heart of the black hole, what they call the 'singularity,' everything breaks down and nothing makes sense," she said, "and because of their faith in their tools and methods, these astronomers are perfectly content to sit with this paradoxical reality. Through their most hard-nosed interrogation, they push themselves into a corner and are left dumbfounded. Wonderful, no?"

She shook her head in awe, at both the singularity and the astronomers who pondered its mystery, I imagined.

"What a difference from the way we in the Humanities behave, coveting our causes and parading our answers when the question itself is barely visible. Compared to these cosmologists, we are like priests obsessing over our holy teeth and bones and splinters of wood in our musty reliquaries. This is why, to get to the point of my dissertation, I've focused on this idea of decadence and farce. I suppose I might have chosen the word 'fetish' to describe this, but I thought 'farce,' from the French 'to stuff,' in the sense of stuffing an animal, as in taxidermy, was much better. What is your opinion on that, Professor? I meant to ask."

But, before I could answer that farce was good, she said, "The way I see it, instead of admitting the existence of a world that fills us with awe and wonder and fear, we've arrogantly hunted down, killed, and skinned that world and are left holding the pelt. The pelt to stretch and mount"—the word taxidermists use for stuffing, I would later discover—"with our theories, until we've stretched them to bursting, until we're sitting with a world full of the stuffing alone."

"I'm not sure where you're going there. Speaking of theories, you'll definitely need to—"

"This is a cosmic shift in our humanity," she said. "We've gone from exploring our inner life, humans' own unknown, the human cosmic singularity, to an endless exhibition of our outsides; the surface, as they say, has become the deepest thing."

"Are you thinking here of the role of social media?"

"It's only the latest step toward this reality, hardly the only, and probably not the last step. What happens when our inner life is vacated, when there is no longer a place to go to work out in private our lives? When the public arena is the place where it is worked out, as spectacle, as farce?"

And, if all that weren't enough, there was still Fritz Haag to ponder, a hundred dollars a bottle, I Googled to learn the next day. The wine, the cheeses, her car, her clothes, the sum of it was a most improbable way for a grad student to live, all made bearable for her survival-dieting art history peers because of how keen she was, I soon discovered, to share her fortunes by hosting the most lavish parties at her spectacularly colorful Eagle Rock apartment with its assorted mix of furniture and art: a down couch upholstered in a patchwork of fabrics, like a Quaker quilt, several ornate Moroccan candleholders hanging from the rafters. She owned half a dozen painted Russian icons that, at this point, might've been originals, and ornate vases fashioned from super-large-caliber artillery casings; trench art, they were called, what soldiers made from refuse strewn across the battlefield during the First World War. Her table runners brimmed with objects of indigenous craft from across the globe, all in keeping with the dishes she'd cook up: Hungarian mushroom soup, a paprika bomb, or a Peruvian dish with black olives and chicken in a green mole, accompanied by a pink-colored rice from Madagascar; an Afghan dish called lamb Kabuli, using a masala of cloves, bay leaf, cardamom, and cinnamon, which she served on a platter big enough to double as a sewer cap: Enjoy, my friends!

Ah, how she'd keep the party going, filling glasses with wine or an aperitif of scotch and limoncello or the most delicious tawny ports, paired with, for instance, a filo dough bird's nest into which she'd spooned chopped walnuts drizzled with syrup. She loved to cook, but, more importantly, loved what a happy belly did for our moods, for the good humor of the human race. As we retired to her living room, she put on music she'd curated but few of us had ever heard, and presently dropped the hostess-with-the-mostest to snatch a dubious idea or opinion drifting about the room and place it under her magnifying glass. "Can any of these writers, I wonder, bring themselves to raise their children believing what they've written?" "What's the point of the gold medal if you're left morbidly cynical of the race." "How casually we endorse this nihilism, no?" And sometimes, I thought, she'd bring that magnifying glass to bear on a problem with the fearless aim of reducing it, and her interlocutors, to cinders, only to have that lethal beam turned back on her. As during one small graduate seminar on Shakespeare's tragedies, with some of the best students in the department, when we were discussing *Macbeth*, a play harboring a good deal of sexism, which hardly meant we should throw it out, because if we did we'd have to throw out three-quarters of the Western canon.

"Elizabethan England was one thing, but complaining about these things like sexism is still alive and well here in America," Sophia said, "is like acting there is a drought when in fact water is sloshing beneath our feet."

Beneath the desk, there was some distinct shuffling of those feet.

"All this complaining is tiresome," Sophia said. "Who doubts women have struggled, but to make like men have been reclining on their ottomans barking orders to their mistresses and wives is a sheer hallucination only Americans could mistake for reality."

"Men lying around? They've been too busy grabbing power," said Daniel, cinching up his ponytail, as though ready for a fight.

Sophia, incredulous: "And what does it mean to 'grab power' anyway? Everyone is grabbing for power as naturally as they grab for water when they are thirsty."

Daniel said, "Don't be evasive. You know what kind of power I'm talking about." He was pale and easily agitated and suffered from a certain super-sweating condition called hyperhidrosis.

"Every time a woman steps into high heels and dolls up or slips into short shorts or even flips her hair, she is announcing her power," Sophia said.

"Now, now, Sophia," said Hannah, a forty-year-old self-identified butch dyke with spiky blue hair.

"Speaking of which, Hannah, how about the power of motherhood. Is it not self-evident we are one and all first and foremost at the mercy of our mothers?"

"As if fathers aren't a force." This was Kimber, an extremely bright Latina and self-identified chola, who wore blackish lipstick, big hoop earrings, and had her hair pulled back and tied up with a red bandana. Her master's proposal was on wall and door graffiti on Echo Park bathroom stalls.

Sophia: "Sure, sure, but for the first five years of a child's life a father's main job is to work, pace about, and submit lofty slogans. Fathers jump into the game late, no? When they're around at all these days."

Daniel: "But when they do jump in, the game is over."

"What do you mean when they're around at all? Who are you talking about?" asked Malika, rearing up in her seat. In her second year, she was the only black student in our program.

Sophia: "Something like a third of households these days are single-parent. Mostly women run. About half of black households are without a father."

Malika: "Well, when they thrown in jail for bagging an ounce, sure, structural racism is going to keep us from comin' home." She was a Columbia grad whose father was a sociology professor. The focus of her recent research was the transformation of the alleged murderer and probable rapist Snoop Dog to his current incarnation as a Rastafarian, and she'd occasionally channel the persona of a gangsta. "Truth, these prisons are like hoarders' houses, 'sept what they hoardin' be niggas."

Sophia: "Probably for the better they're put away anyway, no, Malika? Because male energy is so toxic. But I'm not arguing why it happens, only pointing out women possess extraordinary power to shape a child's consciousness."

Daniel: "Whatever about fathers. Men, or more particularly, white men, have a death grip on power, obviously. That's where the buck stops. Why we call it the patriarchy."

Sophia: "Such a tired slogan."

Daniel: "Tired?"

Sophia: "Women's advantage is everywhere in America and growing every year. And probably when the patriarchy did exist it was men's demand, you might call it revenge, over women for the psychic burden of having to settle down. What a disaster civilization is for men, especially monogamy."

"Say what?" Malika said.

Sophia: "Men are wanderers and adventurers by nature, sexual and otherwise, no? Why pretend it is not so. What violations to their nature men must endure to make it through a day. Sure, to solve problems on their way to their next exploit, they will pause to build this and that, but especially when they are young, they want to keep moving, and would keep moving, if not for the fact that—"

"—sex is easier to get when they have a wife locked up at home," Hannah added.

Sophia: "There has to be some trade-off. For the family's sake. A man ventures out and brings the fruits of civilization to the doorstep of his wife and family, and the wife must open the door, so to speak, for him and raise the kids. In fact, today, most of the excesses of civilization, let's call them, are made for wives and mothers, to the point that you could say it is a kind of ransom that men pay."

Daniel: "Revenge? And now ransom? What the hell is holding men hostage?"

Sophia: "You know this poem by Cavafy, 'The Second Odyssey'? It's about a middle-aged sailor who, in spite of the wealth and harmony of his life, finds himself restless and pining for adventure:

The happy repose of his home,
Penetrated like rays of joy
The heart of the seafarer.
And like rays they faded. . . .
His old friends, the love
Of his devoted subjects,
The peace and repose of his home
Bored him.
And so he left.

Wonderful Cavafy's simplicity, no?"

"Yes," I said.

She smiled. "This is how the poem ends. I will recite it for you alone, Professor:

He felt he was alive once more,
Freed from the oppressive bonds
Of familiar domestic things.
And his adventurous heart rejoiced
Coldly, devoid of love."

Sophia sighed. "Of course, the sentiment strikes many women as well, myself, for sure, but its reality for men is almost universal, up until arthritis or Alzheimer's sets in."

Daniel took notes longhand, with a number two pencil he'd been twirling madly, and more or less in front of Sophia's face. She watched it for a spell, and said, "The lead in your pencil is slipping out."

Daniel slowed it down and asked, "Devoid of love?"

I said, "It's an unexpected, yet powerful ending, isn't it? Even the attachment to those you love may need to be severed to feel alive."

Sophia: "For me, it helps explain the deep psychology of men. And why, back to civilization, when you walk into any department store for every rack of men's clothes you'll find five aisles devoted to women."

Malika: "Creepy to find a woman mansplaining."

Sophia: "Creepier to find men, I don't know, impaling themselves so casually."

Daniel: "Or find you siding, I don't know, so enthusiastically, with the most outrageous aspects of men."

Sophia: "I wonder if we are prepared for the consequences of demoralizing men this way. Or should I use the word castrating?"

Daniel belly-laughed. "Demoralized? I feel liberated, honestly, from the toxicity of masculinity. I feel free to be who I am without having to live up to some paralyzing expectation. I'm in absolute one-hundred percent agreement with my feminist allies. Give the alternative narratives a chance. Enough of this structural sexism that keeps women down. I have no issue with any of that. In fact, I welcome it. Why, as a woman, don't you?"

Sophia: "Does anyone here know how many American soldiers died in combat during World War Two alone? How about in The Great War, as you call it? The American Civil War?"

Amoli, who was usually painfully cautious of saying anything offensive, the very one with a nose ring and tattoo of a Hindu goddess extending up her right arm and dissolving in a mystical cloud at her shoulder, said, "You mean in all those wars men started?"

Hannah, who'd been balancing back in her chair, now squared up on the table: "Are you suggesting there aren't still inequalities worth fighting for just because so many men have died in wars? How about . . ."

Sophia: "Just because? We're not talking about sprained knees. The answer is four hundred thousand American men died in World War Two. But maybe if you knew there were a few transsexuals or cross-dressers among the fallen, you might find room for a tear or two. I bet you think their deaths were deserved for their ill-treatment of women for so many centuries."

Daniel: "War's always been about men and the SLOG: Sex, Land, Oil, or Gold."

Sophia: "Shame on men? And women are all Mother Teresa? Did you have your ears plugged all the way through high school? The cliquishness and plots for revenge women have refined to an art form?"

Amoli: "Now we're going to equate cliquishness with rape and violence?"

Daniel: "Anyway, it's obvious women have resorted to these behaviors because, historically, these were the only means of power men made available to them."

Hannah: "I can't believe you're reaching back to junior high school for evidence to support your, let me be blunt, misogynistic thesis."

"In Europe," I interjected, "until the monarchies were dissolved, you were more likely to go to war if you were ruled by a queen than by a king."

Daniel: "But hasn't it been demonstrated time and again that when women assume positions in the patriarchy, they fall prey to patriarchal ideology? I mean, isn't war itself so deeply embedded in our masculine-centered world that it seems inevitable, natural even to women?"

I noticed sweat starting to pool in the hollow below his nose.

Sophia guffawed: "Next you'll be telling me that breastfeeding is a creation of the patriarchy."

Samuel, usually Daniel's quieter intellectual sidekick, using me for cover, poked his head out of his foxhole: "I kind of get where Sophia's coming from. Have we gone too far in condemning men? I can see that. Do we need to get rid of the whole idea of men, actually?"

Malika, dropping the ghetto, said, "Not 'til we take another hundred steps forward. Sorry, Samuel. You're not getting any indulgences from me."

Sophia focused on Malika and said, "Imagine how many male bodies were broken building the roads and rail lines and dams and bridges and mining the coal or extracting the oil that powers this civilization we all enjoy?"

Kimber: "You mean the same white male bodies that pillaged the earth and brought the environment to the brink of disaster? That . . ."

"Is it possible to find some middle ground here?" I asked. "Why is everybody going to extremes so casually when there are a hundred steps in between we might entertain?"

Sophia shook her head. "You see, in Europe, we had, and still have, our feminists, but this level of, I don't know, resentment . . . Here, it's like we are less interested in equality than in extracting punitive damages."

Kimber agitated a Tic-Tac from its plastic case and laid it on her tongue, and then passed one over the table to Malika, with the aim, it seemed to me, to break Sophia's rhythm. "Maybe," Sophia said, "Americans are so obsessed with these so-called inequalities because, since the Civil War, they didn't have to pick up the bodies of their husbands and brothers and sons from the fields of war in their own backyards."

Samuel: "What I was trying to say is, shouldn't our discussion go beyond talking about men and women anyway. I mean, haven't we established that gender is so much more fluid?"

Sophia: "Homosexuals used to claim they were the way they were because they had no choice in the matter. Now, you can change your sexual orientation at the drop of a hat. What our sex is, and how we express our sex, are two different things. Watch any boys' and girls' football match: boys putting their bodies on the line for the smallest advantage whereas girls are running away from the ball even if they are shooting for a goal. Am I going to get booted out of school for saying that, Professor?"

"No," I said, "but by the way the argument is shaping up, your classmates here might boot you out of the room. I sense some hostility stirring here. Interesting in a way, I have to confess. Are we still talking about *Macbeth*, I wonder?"

Samuel: "I think *Macbeth* is behind us for the time being, Professor. But Sophia, you're essentializing gender in ways that betray a decade of discourse on the subject." He rattled off in short order a few thinkers Sophia should've read more carefully.

Sophia: "Well, you seem to have no problem essentializing men as monsters, and women as the sweetest peacemakers. Anyway, no serious doctor or scientist would take these thinkers you cite seriously. Sure, we have a hermaphrodite here and there, but, really, do we need to spend so much time worrying over these one-in-a-thousand anomalies? Sometimes I think we come to school only to purge ourselves of common sense."

Hannah: "I feel like I'm briefing a grade school student here, but it's about IDENTITY, Sophia. Obviously different than whether you're born with a vagina or penis. It's almost like you're trying to deny certain identity groups full personhood."

Sophia chuckled. "Full personhood? Ninety percent of us reach the end of our lives having achieved barely fractional personhood. And as for this idea of identity, it grows like crabgrass, no?, and comes from everything we experience, and do not experience, our dreams and wishful thinking. Where you grew up, where you went to church or what language you speak or what food you eat; whether your father loved you or beat you or your mother was an alcoholic or fed the poor on weekends, these and so much more make up your so-called identity, if such a thing exists beyond the fact each of us is God's creation."

Daniel: "I was wondering whether your Catholicism has something to do with your take on this. I'm not prejudiced, but, let's be honest, I mean, you're still part of a religion where only men are recognized as priests."

Sophia: "Yes, I am Catholic, and you are prejudiced, obviously. But my opinion is hardly drawn from some encyclical. Look, most women want a man to be caring and agreeable and full of clever conversation, but when push comes to shove, they want him to cut a path, and make a clearing for her so she might plant a future that will bear fruit, first and foremost the fruit of her children. Are women so angry at men because men are doing less of what they used to do and women are doing more of it?"

"Like they should be sitting at home and knitting?" Amoli had reached her limit, apparently. "You're stuck in the muck aren't you? I don't understand why you're so eager to perpetuate these myths, these systems of harm."

Sophia: "Maybe you are harming reality itself. Especially with these cartoon pictures of men, as though they're all sitting in their high-rises manipulating the markets between fellatio with their secretaries. Anyway, the muck might well be our human condition. Fight against it too much and you might wake up one day to discover it is taking us all under."

The most strident feminist in the class, Zelda, who, as some kind of sexio-political statement, had embraced baldness to the extent that she'd shaved off every visible hair, now rolled her browless eyes: "You don't sound Catholic; you sound really, really bizarre. I'm close to saying dangerous."

"You just said it! Trying to shut her down hardly advances the conversation," I said, rolling my own eyes. "Sophia, it's obvious plenty of people would say you're relying on old stereotypes and tropes. I'm sure you know this. But, on the other hand, what's happened that most of you are so knee-jerk dismissive of her observations and opinions?"

It was getting hot, and not only metaphorically. Amoli unwound a long saffron-colored scarf from her neck and draped it on the table. Hannah, who was sitting opposite her, reached for one end and over the table they played a short game of tug of war. Hannah won and swept the scarf onto her lap.

From the corner of my eye, I saw Malika whisper into Zelda's ear.

I said, "If it has anything to do with the discussion, come out with it you two."

Zelda: "Well, we're wondering, we're not certain where you stand. You're taking Sophia's opinions like you agree with her. Honestly, we're starting to feel what she says is fundamentally dehumanizing."

Her tone was somewhere between censure and genuine surprise.

I felt the professorial force rising inside of me, but, at the same time, a little voice was reminding me I was a man, the very thing, in the minds of many, that had led to all the purported misery. "Call me antiquated, I suppose. I enjoy arguments and detest dogmas. And so should we all. This a graduate seminar, for Pete's sake. What are we here for if not to vet these ideas in an open forum, and not shut each other down, especially with references to our religion? Go ahead." I put my hands out, like a referee gesturing for the boxers to continue.

Daniel turned to Sophia and said, "Okay. What are you talking about, really?"

I now found myself slapping my forehead: "Does everyone who disagrees with you have an ulterior motive, Daniel? Her observations aren't good enough to take at face value?"

Sophia: "What do we humans want? Tell me. Health, happiness, to live a good long life, be educated and enlightened, no?"

Either because it was rhetorical or because to entertain her questions at this point was a kind of treason, no one answered.

Sophia: "In all these respects, today women have the advantage over men. At least here in America."

Zelda: "About effing time."

"You'd think in your world you'd find more men complaining," Daniel said, half-chuckling.

"Maybe they're complaining by getting sicker," I said, "dying earlier and more violently than women.

Sophia: "But, they've had it good for so long,

let them suffer a bit. Or maybe all that toxic masculinity is poisoning them to death."

Zelda pulled out an invisible violin and melodramatically started playing.

Hannah: "'Suffer a bit'? Something like eighty percent of Congress is a middle-aged white male. It's like some Southern plantation owners' convention every time they take a group shot for some bill. Come to think of it, that's about the same percentage women make compared to men in their jobs."

Sophia: "Well, since we are throwing percentages around, middle-aged white men are the most prone to suicide of any group; men in general are over ninety percent of the prison population, and they get twelve percent longer prison time than women do for the same crime. Does that point to systemic sexism against men?"

Silence all around.

Sophia: "And don't women have the right to vote men into office? Are you aware we vote in significantly greater numbers than men, and that when women run for office they are just as likely to get elected as men? Next, you will be telling me women are under men's mind-altering control. How, on the one hand, are women the equal of men, and on the other hand, so prone to being exploited, duped, and even hypnotized by them? How demeaning to women. Am I the only one who sees the strangest irony in this?"

Hannah: "Did you also Google what percentage of the sexual predators and rapists are men versus women? Did you Google the number of women who suffer sexual assaults on college campuses alone?"

Sophia: "The numbers, as everyone knows, are staggering, given that you can count yourself a sexual predator if you so much as whistle at a girl these days. Such a farce, no? I wonder who can survive the sexual litmus test men are now required to pass. How about all our progressive icons? JFK, MLK? Gandhi? Obviously not Clinton and his cigars. I love how Gwendolyn Brooks, such a good writer, described Malcolm X: 'We gasped. We saw the maleness. The maleness raking out and making guttural the air and pushing us to walls.' These words sound almost venomous to our ears now, but Brooks used them in praise."

Malika: "Did you say Gandhi?"

Sophia: "He enjoyed sleeping and even bathing with underage girls, to test his celibacy, he claimed. When he was in his seventies, Mahatma routinely took a pair of teenagers with him to bed. One was his grand-niece."

There was some commotion at the front desk. A man with jeans cinched up by a rope and grime thick as tar covering his arms and half-exposed chest was demanding a seat at the bar. The maître d' was clearly right to refuse the bum service, but he was having no part of it, announcing to the room by hell or high water he was going to enjoy a drink while jabbing a finger at the seat he wanted to take it in. A security detail now joined them, likewise stressing that the bum's dress wasn't up to snuff, whereupon he proceeded to tuck in his shirt and dust his hands of the matter. "Now whuh, huh? Now whuh you gonna say?" he said. "Fact," his civil rights were being violated, and if they didn't *tout suite* show him a seat, by God, he'd flag down the police to lodge a formal complaint and get a lawsuit going the likes of which would cost the restaurant many millions if not shutter Shutters altogether, or so I imagine he imagined. The maître d' picked up the desk phone and speed-dialed a number, probably for guidance. As he did, the bum stood there cheerfully, in fact, posing for a guy to my left, dressed in a slim-fitting rubber-band-colored suit, who was videoing the hubbub with his smart phone. It occurred to me that should the pic or vid hit YouTube, the hotel's angelic standing might be seriously diminished, presumably because a security guard marched over to the rubber band and waved his hands, saying, "Turn it off!" The maître d' looked up from the phone call, asked the bum to wait, and left. I wondered, for some reason, how the rocker was faring, and when I looked to see, the answer was *not very well.* He was shaking his head over the hullabaloo as though his mental stability depended on someone getting a grip on it, so much so that the tender virgin was holding him down in fear he'd presently take matters into his own trembling and tattooed hands.

Watching him, I thought that maybe inside of every man is this fretting and bellowing boy that only by a thousand psychic mouth gags is silenced, silenced until ex-rocker-level exhaustion sets in, until the projection of this exhaustion into every innocuous realm is also exhausted, leaving your lifelong arguments for relevance floating like a few goldfish in the stifled waters of a pond given up for waste on a once lavish estate. Yes, I admitted, a certain murkiness, marking the woeful and rather boring beginning of the end, might henceforth sum up your personhood past a certain age, say, forty-seven, if not for all that had menaced you—the bastards, the dumb decisions, the near-misses, even the god-forsaken places—that kept returning, marching brilliantly toward you across some agonizing and sudden bridge in your brain with their war gear swinging. Like some Pashtuns who for thousands of years learned to feed on weeds and live in caves, these devils have not only surprisingly survived but seemed to have beefed up considerably while waiting for your genes to grow slushy and your faculties to desert you. Witness the hungover way you step into your clothes, though you've been teetotaling for weeks, and descend the stairs to breakfast, the same old oatmeal with a few raspberries or blueberries, whatever seasonal antioxidant it is, tossed in, right before swallowing a couple of pills on the doctor's orders, nothing terribly exotic or toxic requiring an infinity of disclaimers, he assures you, in fact, what nowadays nearly every guy over forty-five takes almost as a prophylactic. Ah, for the wondrous illusions of youth that kept one thinking the next day would be better than the last and the future would redeem the past.

Your thoughts now turned to the wan reception of your last book, *The Sly Hand of Fate in Chaucer's Tales*. In the past, you'd be invited to speak here and there to eager audiences about what you'd written, so patiently divined. Notes of congratulation, pats on the back, a small but meaningful celebration of your years-long slog, in keeping with academic courtesy and comradery, would be observed, but, as though overnight, something had changed. Instead of all that, *The Sly Hand* got nebulous smiles, nervous chuckles. "Read it? Sure, of course, but, but . . . let me see here . . ." I might as well have asked them to babysit my colicky kid for an evening. "As it turns out, I'd love to, but I'm busy that night, too busy writing my own book I will naturally expect you to read, because, after all, what I have to say is revolutionary while what you have to say can't be much better than what you last had to say, which was good but nothing to bust a piñata over." Now watch it, your beating heart, plugged into one of those endless stacks at one of our endless libraries with aisle lights that turn eerily on when you enter and off when you leave, a place, like the reliquary of some monastery hidden high in the Caucasus bereft of all but a few keepers of the faith who speak a tongue all but extinct. Yes, a once proud army of scholars who spent their lives driving to the crux of the matter because they believed with all their might it existentially mattered were now reduced to a few cranky souls slumped over their computers typing something, to what mysterious and backbreaking end, besides their dullest tenure, promotion, or the smallest of small-town fame, who knows, the STEM students looking up from their logarithms quite sincerely ask.

The maître d' had returned with a menu, which he now opened maternally for the bum. He pulled a pair of reading glasses out of his sooty pants pocket and situated them on his rather surprisingly handsome nose, which led me to take stock of his other facial features, just as handsome: piercing green eyes and full lips and a wide, elegantly tapered jaw. It's perfectly plausible that he was a former actor who despite having lost his mind hadn't completely lost his dramatic touch. Leaning forward, he pondered and perhaps puzzled over the menu now—English Pea Mezzaluna, Farro and Corn Soup, Grilled Shishito Peppers and Rogue Smoked Blue—as assiduously as any Hasid might puzzle over the parables of the Baal Shem Tov, before he pointed to this, that, and the other, and then paused, before pointing to one thing more: the twelve-dollar donut? Now, if he'd be kind enough to follow security outside they'd prepare the repast and send him off with what amounted to a five-star doggy bag. The maître d' turned his attention back to us and smiled abstractly: an agreement had been reached, and everyone should return to their decadences without further interruption.

For the moment, until we stepped outside, turned the corner, or cruised past their endless encampments, where in the shadows of a thousand titanic building projects these dispossessed drifted about like sea junk. You could find in Los Angeles no greater performers for the causes of the repressed and transgressed, taking advantage of any opportunity to bring their checkbooks and weird healing arts to alleviate the pain of the most menial bruise and yet when it came to the festering reality of those with no place to rest their weary heads suddenly these same people scurry away in confusion and turn to the most stiff-necked bureaucracy for a solution. After spending twenty years away in the gray monumentality of New Haven and then London, how welcoming at first were LA's dazzling light and breezes so cleansing, verily, they seemed to rinse away my many sins. But after a few years, I was forced to conclude, those breezes were mostly bluster. LA leads the way, I'd hear over and over again, and indeed no city breeds more megalomaniacs who throw the most lavish fundraisers for everything from the sexually disoriented to dwindling delta smelts; studio execs who on one day get behind every bill sponsored by #MeToo, and then sodomize barely legals already warped beyond recognition by their delusions of stardom the next; or directors who fill their every frame with the most sadistically imaginative death machines and yet won't let their kids play with a squirt gun. Or lawyers jacking off to every manner of depravity in their high-rise office suites while drafting contracts to mitigate sexual harassment lawsuits at the studios. Bluster and hypocrisy are the currency of this city, and the currency of this city has become the currency of the entire country, I thought, sitting there with my martini. Or Hollywood parents who lecture their kids on diversity and inclusion but treat their neighborhood schools like the Chernobyl community zoo. How our own sensitivity- and diversity-infused colleagues push their kids at diaper age into this forty-five-grand-a-year academy and that eighty-five-dollar-an-hour tutor, effectively robbing them of what makes the world howl and sing, all to get them some miserable and hypothetical leg up on their peers for that one-time shot at an Ivy or the like. Look at our darlings, existentially massaged to the point of blistering, at this ugliest of cotillion balls in their cute little uniforms for their lame coming out. Look at them towing that most extraordinary dray full of test scores and recommendations and grades, with a few months of some utterly outrageous so-called extracurricular stuffed in—starting a petition to once and for all outlaw foie gras or writing a gender-neutral potty-training manual. Or, fund driving for some impoverished tribe in Guatemala, which, when you actually visit (on your way back from a rave in St. John's with your bros, but still), you contract some weird parasite that produces blood in your cum, a harrowing tidbit, sure, but it turned your college essay into the oddest tearjerker, you tell friends, and probably tipped the scales for you at Yale. Yes, by the time they reach us they are literally bursting at their delicate seams with scenes of injustice while at the same time having suffered themselves not more than being forced to tough it out at Motel 6 for the Coachella Music Fest when they were sixteen. I loathe to see them all full of themselves and at the same time utterly gutted of joy by their guilt over what they enjoy, their brains filled to the brim with the most tendentious theories about others, not to mention their precious thoughts about themselves and their untold potential, which should anyone in the least trample, they drop a thousand neurotic bombs to defend, making them untouchable in terms of reprimand or low grades so that all but a handful of certified goof-offs or dolts get Bs or better.

I recalled my most ruthless and beloved

mentor, Mark Lipsky, now ten years dead, who was the first to introduce me to Broadsides and Ballads, Spirituals and Folk Songs, which he'd made his life's work and which I, for a period, hoped to make my own. Shakespeare, Marlowe, Spenser, and Chaucer, all good, he felt, but let us not forget what is homespun and belted out in shacks and pubs, gambling dens and cotton fields. As we strolled across campus together, he slightly stooped in the way of the tall, which he was, he'd sing some Negro spiritual, dozens of which he knew by heart, among them, "Ho' the wind don't let it blow," or "Before I'd slave oh freedom," or "Dese bones gwine rise again." How inexplicably happy Scottish ditties made him, the very ones where mothers murdered their babies, girlfriends poisoned lovers, demons seduced women, and where sex was everywhere and done with near anyone, as in the "Ballad of Lizie Wan," whose brother discovered he'd knocked her up, and to avoid the scandal, pulled out his wee penknife and cut *her fair bodie in three.* In fact, all songs worth their salt possess a scandalous aspect, he claimed. His mind was fearless, radiant, knitting the most elaborate patterns from the most random threads, but his guidance was so oblique—"you might try this or you might think about that"—I was usually better off not asking for the wild goose chases that ensued. "Dr. Lipsky, I read the entire book and didn't find one mention of . . ." "Well, my sense was you were actually thinking about something else and it was that something else I sent you in search of." I recalled my essay on Child Ballad number 30, how I walked into his office and asked, "Did you get around to reading it, Dr. Lipsky?" "Yes," he said, picking through his massive and messy desk (that by his own admission he hadn't sorted through in months) only to find my twenty-seven-pager near the bottom of some forsaken pile. Flipping through it with a big lone finger, "Hmm," he said, "let me see. Oh, yes. Yes, indeed. Quite predictable, and, I'm afraid to say, callow. You haven't said anything here that hasn't been said a hundred times before and much better." He handed it over to me, as though for recycling, the paper, hardly the ideas. "Well, if I can't help you with anything else, I hope to next see you in class."

I can still feel my chastened body bobbing away from the supertanker he was, clinging to a little ring buoy of obloquies: prick, nitpick, probably too lazy to read it! Okay, say he did read it; say his conclusion was justified, but his delivery, his choice of words—Callow! Predictable!—boomed again and again as I tumbled onto that desiccated island where all battered egos are left to bandage up and take stock. Consider your likeness to the tumbleweeds, how they stir and turn only to gather against a shack up the hill, or to the countless fish surf and wind have scoured to the bone, those the fleas are now finishing off. Oh, pity, pity, pity over your stupid little self, a contraption that a few people had wound up and now sputtered to a benumbed stop at Lipsky's savage door. Admit it: You'd become too satisfied with yourself. Yes, Lipsky was near retirement age, if not a little past it, and yes he'd probably seen hundreds of full-of-themselves students like you come and go until cataracts set in, but such a person is precisely who you need to focus on; you need to focus on this terrifying father figure so you might eventually bring your wobbly person into focus. Yes, sitting there all alone on that island for a good long spell, how strangely invigorating his ruthlessness proved; how nice to be flushed of your every fancy about yourself. What a stroke of luck you'd been given a chance to become something other than what you preposterously imagined you were. How refreshing someone cared enough about what they were doing to not worry themselves over your fidgety little ego, or your so-called feelings. "Your feelings are perfectly irrelevant," Lipsky might say. "What is at stake is our understanding of ourselves without recourse to anything but ourselves. A revolutionary quest. Do you realize the sacrifices we've made to cut a path through all this ignorance! What do your feelings matter, when excommunication, jail, torture, censorship, and, most common and perhaps most devastating of all, sheer apathy is what our writers and artists and scientists have for five hundred years faced in order to paint for us this most amazing panoramic view of the human condition?"

Zeke came back around, and so I ordered my second martini and asked to see the bar menu—perhaps these memories of my mentor had opened my appetite. Or maybe it was because I hadn't eaten but a piece of toast since morning. The sea bass ceviche sounded good.

"Are you expecting someone?" he asked.

"She should be coming soon."

"Should I put down another place setting?"

"Why don't you."

No sooner had he left than my thoughts pivoted to one fall break when I suggested that Sophia and two other foreign students similarly far from home join me in the desert for Thanksgiving dinner. After my divorce, I bought near Palm Springs a house on an outsized lot, large and soon well-appointed enough to entertain two or three friends at a time. I intended my desert pad to be a retreat, but its seductions were too strong to resist, and after a year I found myself squeezing my classes together so I could stay out there longer and longer and hike deeper and deeper into the nearby Joshua Tree National Park, with its biblical-looking upside down trees and enormous boulders stacked with impossible and haunting precision two stories or more high. How blissfully mysterious was the desert, with its monumental patience and haunting spells of tranquility, and at night its endless cicadas and pulsing ocean of stars. Time and again it gobbled me up, spit me out, and quieted me down. You come to an age, which I had apparently reached, when you want to be rid of yourself and make room for something cosmically more. But what?

As an answer, perhaps, I petitioned the state prison in Chino to open a weekly two-hour course introducing inmates to Shakespeare. What a frustrating number of forms I was made to fill out, waiting and waiting for the course day and hour and reading material and format, hardback or soft, and even paper and pencil to be approved. The prison offered numerous classes but only a few, like mine, were considered an elective, so I hoped those who showed up would do so for the love of learning and not just to check off one more box en route to securing a GED. And here they came, twelve in all, shuffling in and slipping into their bolted-down chairs around the bolted-down table. I remember how the room seemed to physically contract from the gravity of their hemmed-in masculinity and yet how mentally supple and attentive they were. They ranged in age from eighteen to seventy-two, and included, I would in time discover (I didn't dare ask up front), drug pushers and multiple drug offenders, a burglar, a serial identity thief, an arsonist, and several serving time for assault with a deadly weapon. I passed out paperback copies of *Lear* (hardcovers make decent cudgels) and started in, omitting for the time being where I taught, where I earned my degree or my motivation for being there. What else besides my name did they need to know, and, frankly, what more did I need to know about them; with our varying degrees in criminality, we were each there to let Shakespeare lead the way.

It was slow going, every line required painstaking translation, Elizabethan English as familiar to them as Estonian. But they kept with me, and I with them, week to week—when there wasn't a lockdown or one or another wasn't getting called up to court or a visit with a relative—until I saw the spark in their eyes, a smile, a nod, until they were savoring the Bard's mad genius, how he renders evil, greed, and pride, the mind's obsessive stratagems to swindle or outwit, and madness, oh, madness, how we barely see it coming as it barrels toward us, how a thousand seemingly trivial blows to the head or one massive slam leaves one wandering the wastelands imploring the gods of lightning and thunder for justice and revenge.

We are meant for stories, built for them. They create a safe space where we might ponder who we are and what is in store by not having to look at ourselves or life head-on. But to truly absorb the truths of the giants, we must, in the end, confess our complicity if not our very direct participation in these crimes of the heart and mind, I told them. Yes. They'd been there; they'd seen that; they'd been that! No strangers either to the catastrophic consequences.

And yet, and yet, they had relationships, girlfriends, and mothers, and trades, training horses or building motorcycles, and homes, a cabin in Alaska or a double-wide in Texas, all waiting for their asthmatic persons to breathe new life into. And justification too, for why, even after reading Shakespeare, a rotten judge, a lazy lawyer, a lying cop had landed them in the shit can. "If only the world could stand for a second in my shoes!" How strange it was to discover how victimized those who victimized others felt, their criminal acts a settling of scores against a world that had turned its back on their own injuries and misery. The criminal mind is the most common kind of mind, like all minds hostile to self-reckoning, convinced of its rectitude, justified by the deep sense of injustice it suffered, sometimes against its very nature. "Okay, I did push against the fences, but, man, look, how monotonous and boxed in they make you feel. Probably, when I get out, I'm going to climb right over one again, go back to doing what I was doing before, because it's in me, I don't know why, man, in me to get my chunk on the cheap." Ah, everybody wants their chunk on the cheap, I thought, all because the mind loves its twisted shortcuts too much. We are all abetted in our thought crimes by the same self-satisfying system, the one in our skulls, the one that turns mere correlation into causation, accident into agency, complexity into simplicity, and our most ridiculous idiosyncrasies into the most obvious universalities. Poor reality. It could barely recognize itself if it came face-to-face with the human mind's version of it. Look how the most objective scientists embrace the most ludicrous voodoo when swamped by love, hate, or best of all, fear. This recognition of the human mind, the implacably dark, refractory features of it is what has been trivialized, I thought, thinking back to my mentor, Lipsky. "The great artistic works, whether written or sung, are windows onto the outrageous nature of the human condition," Lipsky once told me, and now, I thought, we've shuttered these windows and instead nailed political tracts on the inside of our bolted-down doors. Alas, how oblivious we've grown to the brute nature of reality and the herculean coping mechanisms we must almost nonstop employ to keep it from withering us from the inside out. These ideologues are willfully oblivious of how nearly every thought is a molestation of reality, how nearly every thought is worked over to the point of high art to merely dovetail with the thought that came before it. How patently absurd our arguments look at the exact moment when we believe they have triumphed.

But back to that Thanksgiving break. The German and Argentinian students who were coming together decided to drop out at the last minute, but Sophia was intent on following through with the meal she planned for the four of us. Since she was cooking, I wanted to buy the ingredients, a big mistake, as her list was a page long, and included items that took me all the way across the county to fetch. I should have known: She would never balk at the effort it would take others to do whatever it was she decided because she would not balk at the effort it would take her to do whatever it was they had decided. She would never say to herself, "Well, I should be more considerate of the time it will take this poor soul," but rather would think, "these people need to get pushed away from all these routines they find so friendly, anyway."

She arrived early in the morning in tennis shoes and jeans and a big fluffy white sweater, and with me as her sous chef we started in; first, on that turkey that was stuffed with that deboned goose and that goose that was stuffed with that deboned pheasant because, she explained, there is no more boring a bird than turkey all by itself—even the Bourbon Red heritage variety (what she ordered) is nothing terribly special. The caster sugar, somewhere in texture between powdered and regular sugar, she melted, along with butter and turkey stock, to make a gorgeous glaze for those chantenay carrots; the sweet batard, essentially a baguette, I discovered, she cut up into small perfect squares for the prune and apple and venison sausage stuffing that took a hundred small steps to perfect. She was a force to be reckoned with in the kitchen, the four-star general—muscling open the back end of those birds was something to behold—barely waiting for me to get out of the way to reach for the cutting board or mallet or as she marched toward the sink.

We talked and drank, politics and prosecco in the kitchen, philosophy and chablis on the porch, and then, back in the kitchen, we opened a split of pinot noir for the finishing touches.

"The way you pile on the butter. My arteries are hollering just watching you."

"Well," she answered, "if you think they will holler they probably will. Butter is gold for the body. In fact, whatever has been used to cook for centuries is gold for the body, no matter what the doctors say."

It is the speed at which we eat, she claimed, and the fact we don't take the time to cook the way we used to cook that is making us fat, because notice how when you cook you are already half satisfied by the time the dish hits your stomach; and how good food tastes when time is taken to prepare it, how you savor each bite, and how contented you feel after just a few.

"Fast food and all of this never truly satisfies. Like internet sex versus great lovemaking, no?

Americans use food to push down their vexations. When they eat, they are attending to everything but their bodies. This country is full of vexations. Everyone so panicked they will die they die from the panic itself. For a place with so many freedoms how weighted down Americans are by their complaints and anxieties. Since it is Thanksgiving, it makes me wonder if Americans' fear is actually fear of each other, the consequence of a country made of tribes that have come together by way of some delicately constructed truce that might at any second fall apart. It is incredible this country has survived. A place where there is no faith in tradition, in the past, to help bridge the differences. Everything here is contested to the point of farce, including, nowadays, Thanksgiving. Well, should we sit?"

We did, and toasted our efforts, and then she asked if she might pray. Before I could say yes, she reached around with her hands and I gave her my own, our arms making a full circle around the fare. "Father in heaven, Creator of all and source of all goodness and love, receive our heartfelt gratitude this Thanksgiving Day. Thank you for the food and shelter, our health, the love we have for one another, our family, and friends, AND mentors, all the graces and blessings that sustain us. In the name of Jesus, your son and our brother, Amen."

"Dig in, and thank you for the mention of 'mentors.' I'm sure that wasn't included in the official prayer."

"Well, I am thankful for you. What a gift to have such a patient and intelligent teacher."

"Not so patient, but the other I'll take."

She now wanted me to try something special she picked up from a shop in Glendale, an Armenian varietal called Areni from the winegrowing region of the same name. As she filled our glasses, she explained how they'd been growing grapes in this region forever, but only recently did they discover a winery there, some 6,100 years old, where winemaking probably began.

"The same as it was back then, this wine is fermented in amphoras," she said, "clay vessels. You can taste it, right?"

I couldn't, though it was undeniably delicious, as was the food it was playing off of, the oily and earthy richness of that foul concoction, the herb-infused lusciousness of that stuffing and the delicate firmness of those sweeter than sweet carrots.

"I was a week in Armenia, with my father, on one of his many junkets. I saw many marvelous things there, but one eyeful of Ararat would've been enough."

"Where Noah landed."

"Once you see it you know it will be the last thing standing, two large overlapping triangles, composed on the most perfect of plains. It was the crossing road and regular crushing point of empires for some three millennia, Armenia was. They have these ancient stone churches carved out of mountains or perched on the edge of cliffs or at the bottom of ravines, their sturdy geometry having withstood centuries of human and natural storms. How disgraceful, no?, to watch these worlds honed to precision by thousands of years of fire and ice heaped into the great global mulch pile. How is it in an age that prides itself on diversity, everywhere we turn we are losing the subtleties of cultures, their almost unfathomable fullness, losing it for the same unbearable sameness."

"At the same time, everywhere we turn our differences are weirdly magnifying. And we're at each other's throats, losing the subtleties of interpretation and perspectives."

"Ironical, no? Maybe we hate what we see in the mirror."

"Let's move to the living room. Honestly, I feel like a version of our turkey."

I already had the fireplace going. She took my leather swivel lounger to the side of it, flipped her shoes off, lay her legs over the armrest, and turned her eyes to the big picture window.

"The darkness is amazing out here," she said, "so absolute, if not for the stars. I imagine when there is a cloud cover you can't see ten feet in front of you."

"Part of the reason I love it here. You can disappear."

But I needed to hit the john and excused myself.

As I stepped into the bathroom, no more than five yards away, I heard her say, "You would have me tonight if I decided to, no?"

Her syntax sparked a spasm all the way from my head to my groin. Had I heard her right? Unsure, I made as though I hadn't heard her at all. "If I decided to." To what? Make love? From nerves, the shit flushed out in a flash. "Have me." It's an innocent idiom, idiot! As in, "I'll have you over for dinner soon." My head felt like a pinball machine some high-schooler was having a drunken whirl at. Speaking of drunk, I was getting there, if not positively there, and so, maybe, was she, what could very well explain her tortuous arrangement of words. But why, if so innocent, had she waited until I stepped away to ask it? To give me time to think it over? Say I did have her, the way deep down I'd die to 'have' her, and somehow they found out. Sitting on the john, which had suddenly turned into some kind of interrogation chair, my rebuttal sounded shadily rehearsed:

"It was dark out, and we'd been drinking, for God's sake! Did you want me to demand she drive home after she asked to stay? What if she'd gotten injured on the road?"

Brushing all that aside: *"Did you have a sexual encounter with her?"*

"We are friends. Whatever happened between us is none of your business."

"Then the answer is 'yes.'"

"Yes, yes, but it was mutual!"

"Mutual?"

"She's a grown woman! With a grown woman's natural appetite, I might add. There is nothing illegal going on here, if that's what you're implying."

"What is illegal and what is unacceptable are two different things. We should think we've made this point clear by now: Haven't we made clear the institutional power differential at work here? Isn't it obvious, your implicit leverage over her?"

"But she approached me! Might I even dare say she had leverage over me? Have you bothered to take a look at her?"

"Where institutional power differentials exist, it

is impossible for a woman to consent."

"I'm trying to tell you; she drew me to herself for a kiss!"

At this juncture, I was going vaguely insane. Put her out of your brain! They're right. She is your student! Even if she's game tonight, she might call foul tomorrow, or a year from now, or two. The black tar of regret can bubble up out of nowhere, and with lethal consequences. A fuck, a suck, a fondle, a lick, even too insistent a stare, does not occur, slip into the past, recede from consciousness, and eventually drift into oblivion, no, it lives and relives in the deepest layer of our brain, in an eternal present, where, by the way, there is no statute of limitations.

"Believe me, she was into it."

"'Into it' is impossible. There are only so many levels of unawareness, which we have time and again sought to make you perfectly aware of."

"Please."

"And now that you've pushed us to it, let us also make you aware of this: Sex between a man and a woman is rarely, if ever, an encounter among equals, it almost always involves a quotient of power if it is not the rawest expression of power per se. To put it in layman's terms, terms you might understand: Men shaft women in innumerable ways."

Even so . . .

Let her ask again. This time around she'll make her intentions clear. Then again, what if she didn't ask again, and I'd squandered the chance to make love to this once-in-a-lifetime lover? Let's look at it from this angle: Could you possibly make love to this woman without falling in love? One go-around with her might be enough to cripple you forever. Every man is looking to find the flawless composite; from all the facets of women, the single perfect woman is invented. When that woman, beyond one's wildest dreams, incarnates and is actually there for the taking, when the archetype itself is staring into your eyes and sitting on your dick, there is no coming back from it. When she is gone, when she invariably slips away, you are left shattered, infantilized, hypnotized, repeating her reality for eternity in your brain. For this fact alone, the Trojan war got roaring. The psychic wall you'd so fastidiously engineered between the two of you since the first day she walked into your class was crumbling before your middle-aged eyes. Let's face it, you'd left holes in your wall, hadn't you? Hoping she'd someday hop through.

I took a step into the hallway and stood at the threshold, studying her as she looked out the window. I admitted, without fear, for the first time, really, admitted without reservations the crushing absoluteness of her beauty, the perfect curve of her neck, and the wave over wave of her hair, glowing in the light of the flames like flames themselves.

"Brown stars, yellow dwarf stars, red giants; so many different kinds," she said, apparently sensing I was there.

"What's that?" I said, and went to the kitchen for some water, in the largest glass I could find.

"I was saying how I love the Sesame Street names these astronomers come up with. White dwarf. It is a dead star, a pure carbon corpse, a diamond the size of a planet."

I filled up a pitcher and took it with me, along with two glasses, back to the living room.

"I think I'm in the hydrating phase of the evening," I said.

"Yes, I have quite a drive home, apparently, so I should probably water up too."

Keep your focus, fool. Yes, she did say "apparently"! Have mercy on yourself!

I nonchalantly poured her a glass and took my place back on the couch.

She swiveled the chair so that she was facing me.

But should I sit or lie down? I fidgeted for a bit, before deciding I better do the former.

"Are you okay, Professor?"

"Maybe a little overstuffed."

"It was an extravagantly rich meal."

"But you were talking about Sesame Street."

She sat up and tucked her legs beneath her. "About the childlike names astronomers give the stars. Even their telescopes: There is The Very Big Telescope, and the European Extremely Large Telescope and the Very Small Array in Chile," she chuckled. "It is used to detect cosmic microwaves generated from when the universe was born. Amazing the mass we can observe and measure is in no way adequate to generate the gravity necessary to hold the universe together. No, something is happening out there we can only call dark for how much in the dark we are about what it is. A miracle we do not either fold in on ourselves or fly apart. Some force is holding it all together, just so."

And you'll need to muster all the dark energy and dark matter you possess to hold yourself together. Do it. "Just as much a miracle was that meal you made. Since Poles are hardly famous for their cuisine, I was wondering where you learned."

"Naturally, on those trips with my father."

"Diplomatic missions."

"Yes, to Istanbul, or Buenos Aires, Brazil; Alexandria and Mumbai. I experienced the aromas and tastes and textures of food from all over the world, especially so-called street foods, which I sampled with or without my father, because, though he made me promise I'd stay indoors and study, I always snuck out."

"I imagine you were a handful. Still are."

"Fathers are important for daughters, maybe more important than they are for sons. That is why this attack on fathers we find everywhere in the media today is so disturbing. Some wise woman always bringing the babyish dolt around to the right point of view. I tell you, when fathers are mistrusted or turned into babyish dolts, every form of authority looks suspicious."

"You had a good relationship with your father, then," I said.

"I was a troubled teenager and made his life crazy. From when I was young, I confess, I deliberately looked for opportunities to practice a kind of creative destruction. The reason I love cooking, I suppose. The way things transform, bathed in fire the way they cancel and blend, equalize and vaporize, and are born again."

"I thought this creative destruction, as you put it, was a part of your personality, not something you deliberately practice."

"I began to practice it deliberately, but only

after I was forced into it by necessity or even fate."

"How's that?"

"It is a long story, but when I was thirteen years old, I had an experience on the steps of St. Mary's, where our Polish Pope, John-Paul, once presided, that changed me to this day. You see, we were a traditional Catholic family, the only type of religion communism tolerated."

"Outside of the religion of communism itself, you mean."

"So true, so true. Anyway, I was fervent in my beliefs, especially as a child, mesmerized by images of the Virgin cradling her baby, and thirty-three years later, her baby hanging on the Cross. That day, we had finished Mass, and I had stepped outside in my pretty little blue-and-white Sunday dress. It was June and sunny with a breeze, and my parents and uncles and aunts were hugging friends, and my little cousins were milling about waiting for them and I was left to myself, wondering about the homily, about heaven and hell, wondering whether I'd ever know the many sins hiding inside of me and what would come of me if I failed to root them out, when a terrible feeling fell upon me, a dark cloud so ominous I was instantly gripped by a paralyzing fear. I know, it sounds like something out of a nineteenth-century potboiler, but there it was, darkness, swallowing me up, me crying on the steps of the church, and my parents and relatives one by one coming over to see what was wrong with this girl, never at a loss for words, who was now pushing them away so violently. That I couldn't get a handle on my emotions petrified everyone, so they took me home and immediately called our doctor, a man I knew my entire life. After speaking with my parents for several minutes, he came into my bedroom alone and asked, 'What is wrong, Sophia? You are a healthy girl. Your parents assure me you are eating well and your energy has been good. Nothing seemed wrong, until this afternoon.' 'I don't know what is wrong. It's just that, suddenly I felt a sickening horror all the way through me, from my head to my toes.' 'Did someone do something to you? Have you done something you regret?' 'No, doctor. Everybody is good to me. Nobody has done me anything wrong. It is me, myself, and I that I regret. Everything about me.' 'Nonsense,' he said. 'You are a wonderful girl, not perfect, of course, but if you were perfect, you would have no need to grow and learn.' Our doctor patted me on the shoulder, rose to his feet with a sigh, and left. I had started my period months before, and it could be hormonal stress, he reasoned. After giving my parents some anti-anxiety medicine, he asked to see me again in a week, when, if my situation did not improve, he would send me to a psychiatrist."

"Did you improve?"

"Yes and no. As soon as I took the medicine, my hysteria disappeared, but what took its place was a hollowness, a hollowness that attracted the most terrible thoughts, toward others and myself, blood and torture, mayhem, dismemberment, and death, in my dreams and daydreams, in hundreds of cartoons I made, men freefalling from buildings, women drowning in acid, and body parts strewn over an abandoned factory lot, of people leaving church toting their heads in their hands. Something violent had been done to me, and I saw it everywhere now. And then, one day, I caught a glimpse of what that something violent was. I was doing my studies when my mother called me for dinner; I got up to go, but suddenly I knew it was not me that had gotten up to go but some double of myself."

"A doppelgänger?"

"Not exactly, but in a second I will explain. At dinner, I realized how I was doing everything expected of me, but again, this double was doing it. It was frightening at first, but soon I trained my mind to watch this double dispassionately, watch it respond to an endless series of commands, at school, at church, at home. And then it dawned on me: What I felt on the steps of the church, what horrified me, was the completion of a nearly invisible process occurring since I was a toddler. A transposition, thirteen years or so in the making, was complete. Yes, the subtly violent apparatus of society had finally accomplished its work, my double, this perfect and pleasant machine whose sole purpose was to give birth to yet another generation of perfect and pleasant machines, was complete. When during college I learned the word simulacrum, I turned it into *sickalacrum* to describe what I'd become."

"So that's where it comes from." It was a neologism she applied to significant effect in her dissertation.

"All writing is autobiographical. I'm hardly the first to say it. Yes, without the most shattering violations against every square inch of our persons, civilization would not exist. Civilization, its horrors, but also its so-called beauty and riches, all of it is premised upon making a *sickalacrum*, a catastrophe of our persons, a universally sanctioned and perfectly rationalized assemblage of violations. Violations I would eventually need to violate, but who would show me how?"

"Not the church, obviously."

"But Jesus is a different matter. The Catholic church is one of many mediums through which His grace works. But you are right, at the time I had to turn for guidance elsewhere, and so I found my first and most satisfying mentor in Dostoyevsky, a man who refused to orphan any of his thoughts, who, in fact, took delight in expressing them to the shock of those who dared listen. His irrefutable command of language, the clarity and cosmic scale of his consciousness forced you to confront how hard you've worked to close your own consciousness of these violations down. I've often wondered what great writers have in common since their styles and temperaments can differ so widely; I think, when it is all said and done, great writers somehow free people from the neurotic energy spent in pushing their tabooest thoughts away. Being decent and temperate is at its root hostile to the evil genius of all that is great and true, of all great writers. Decency is something each of us can at least in the hypothetical reach, whereas true genius strikes us as unreachable from very early on. Because we cannot reach it our reflex is to revile it unless, of course, we manage to harness the genius of others for our own profit. The most intelligent people, first, will hate you for daring to have thoughts they haven't thought or better thoughts they hadn't the courage to entertain much less enjoy the disorienting powers of. I knew this all in my heart, so, I began devouring Dostoyevsky, devouring Rimbaud and Apollinaire and especially Artaud, and later Burroughs and your Bukowski, anything I could get my hands on that might aid me in my most terrible program, which I accomplished, at first, without too much protest from my parents because at the same time I achieved this program alongside a flawless academic record. But, by sixteen, no matter how well I was doing in school, I was pushing the envelope, as they say. The wound is the place where the light enters you, Rumi said, but I was prying it open by any means available, staying in pubs until two a.m., smoking Russian cigarettes and taking dangerous girlfriends and then disappearing from home for two or three days at a time, until, enough was enough, and my mother demanded my father take charge. I was traveling with him a lot, but now for longer and longer, including the entire summer break. What an irony it was on one of those junkets I met my first lover, in Macedonia, where my father was scheduled to stay for a month, using Skopje as a base for his work in the other former Yugoslav republics. I was at my favorite café reading Robert

Walser when I noticed sitting across from me a wonderfully handsome man in corduroy slacks and cardigan with stylish eyeglasses reading the paper and drinking an espresso. I watched him for I don't know how long, but I couldn't keep staring forever, so I went back to Walser, wondering now what occupied the handsome man's mind, what brought him to that table this morning, looking so intelligent and debonair. When I looked back up, he was gone. I was wondering what direction he'd taken home when I felt a tap on my shoulder. He was smiling and asking something about my hair. My Macedonian was so-so, but before long we settled on English, which I spoke well, and my soon-to-be friend spoke well enough. He said he needed to let me know how much he admired the color of my hair, the almost exact color of a glass of wine he had enjoyed the night before. 'A Vranac,' he said. I later learned it was an important grape in that region."

I could see it myself. "In a certain light, your hair is the deepest reddish brown, almost going on purple, isn't it," I told Sophia.

"You've noticed. My grandmother's hair, strange for a Pole, but there it is. 'Do you mind if I smell it?' he asked. 'Of course not,' I told him. 'Does it smell like your wine?' I asked, and he said, 'No, it smells like springtime, in the vineyard where the grapes for that wine are grown.' 'And how are you so familiar with this vineyard?' I asked, and he said he owned it, in Tikves, and would I like I could come to his home for lunch and taste the most recent vintage. I already ate, so fearless, I said, 'Of course, but only the wine,' and we walked a mile or so up to his house, a building with roses creeping up the side of a stone wall and a most wonderful but old dog, with long straight hair that fell over his big eyes like some hippy from the sixties, greeting us as we entered through a gate into a little courtyard with a fountain. It was a Lhasa Apso, he told me, an ancient and sacred breed that lived inside Tibetan monasteries, to warn monks when danger came near. As he left to get the wine, I played with the dog, and soon he returned with two glasses, a small plate of feta and olives, both of which he had made and cured himself. We toasted the day, and he asked questions politely, smiling at my answers, trying to gain my confidence, naturally. You must have at least a hint you are being seduced for the seduction to reach its most delicious pitch. With that said, after a couple of hours getting to know each other, or rather, he got to know me, he said he had to get going and walked me back to the café."

"You've got me hooked."

"Every morning I went to the same café to the same table, like an incantation, a magic spell I imagined would produce the same results, but after a week of doing this, I lost hope. I could have found out if he was married or had a girlfriend if I hadn't been so busy blabbing about myself, but my vanity had gotten the best of me and left me, as it almost always does, in the dark. There is nothing more tempting, is there, than the self and all its foggy pomposity to turn to when one is feeling small, when in fact, the self is really the start of the end of everything that makes life magical and big, unless one can develop the rare ability to observe it with the calmest curiosity and not take too seriously its demands to be taken seriously. In any case, I thought maybe I should go to his home, but I was embarrassed to reveal my desire so nakedly, and then I thought, no, this is exactly what you must do. 'The shame of your desire is what is shameful,' I told myself. After getting prettied up, I walked to his house and went through the gate into the courtyard where the fountain was playing and knocked on the door. He opened it smiling: 'Hello, Sophia!' Now, what would I say, besides 'hello' back? 'Please come in,' he said. 'Did you leave something behind?' Instantly, I knew there was no woman in his life. The kitchen I stepped into was disheveled in a way men leave things disheveled when they have no woman looking out for them. 'I wanted to see the inside of your home. I've been wondering about it since we had that glass of wine.' 'I should have invited you in last week,' he said, 'Come.' 'You live alone?' I asked. However certain I was about it, I needed confirmation, because I felt if he was going to be my first lover then at least I must be the only one in his life at the time. 'Yes,' he said, 'three years now.' 'I could tell from your kitchen,' I said, showing my catlike attentiveness.

"In his sitting room, the windows were set deep into the walls, letting the softest light in. Just as soft was the music, Mahler, I believe, he had playing. Books and records and objets d'art were everywhere, on a dozen or more bookshelves, but also stacked on the floor against the walls, and on end tables and his coffee table. I remember being struck by the warmth and peculiar harmony of his world, a kind of relaxed, masculine order beneath all the surface disorder. I was getting relaxed now myself, and asked if he had wine for me, and as he went to the kitchen, I continued looking about. 'Where is your dog?' I asked, when he returned with the wine, in a beautiful crystal glass. 'Lydia? I believe she is napping.' '*Na zdravye*,' he said, 'cheers,' and we toasted. 'Did she have a long night?' 'She is old and sleeps half the day, but her spirits were so brightened by your last visit,' he told me. In his library, around the corner, I had noticed an antique wooden cabinet with a large lock, and I asked him what was in it. 'Firearms,' he said, 'I've collected them since I was a boy.' 'For hunting?' 'Wherever and however I might need them,' he said. 'Do you not like hunting. Sophia?' 'In fact, I do not approve of hunting as sport alone. Killing for the challenge of the chase and so on.' But I was determined to keep him the topic of conversation, and so I asked him a few more questions as I drank, hoping to break through my doubts and reach a most happy buzz before our lovemaking commenced. 'Let me show you,' he said, and left the room for a few seconds and returned with one of those old iron keys. He had about fifteen rifles and handguns in the cabinet, and many were amazingly ornate, and with great stories, I soon discovered. 'They are objects of ingenuity and beauty, machines that changed as certainly as did the printing press the course of human history.' He had me handle a few of the rifles, to get a sense of how they felt, cradled against the body, and then asked, 'Would you like to see Lydia again?' He took my hand and led me down a hallway. 'Let's tip-toe,' he told me, 'to not wake her.' We did wake her, of course. On his bed, step by gentle step he proceeded to open me up. I resisted, of course, first this, then that, resisted as one must resist, to measure the intensity of your lover's desire for you, the truth and depth of his feelings. 'No,' I said, to assert my power over him, 'no,' to sin without sinning because, yes, there was still some Catholic in me. He was a very patient lover, and for the next several weeks he showed me how to find pleasure in the most unexpected places and ways. It is one thing to gallivant with boys your own age but entering the mysteries of an older man is to confront an unspeakable truth about your desire."

"Speaking of older men. Did your father know? Did he find out?"

"Of course not, though he may have sensed something had changed, a deepening and at the same time leveling off of my personality that of course is one of the surest signs of sexual maturity. But I was going to say something else. I found sex was the key by which I could inch back into myself, be relieved of myself by bringing joy to my partner. I learned the power I possessed, the power to awaken a man's flesh, to heat up desire, to quench it and make it thirsty again, desire, an endless wave of it, desire as the existential constant, let's say, women possess the innate power to satisfy. Why doesn't anyone talk about this reality when they talk about power? Let's face it: No number of PhDs can equal what women possess quite naturally. All men know they are ultimately disposable and if push came to shove nature would need only a handful of them to populate a village. Even moose hunters are prohibited by law to kill cows and calves, while it is open season on bulls, especially when they are rutting." She laughed. "Mother tongue, mother culture, mother nature, mother earth. Next to all that is your poor Father Time, which all men feel is running out on them."

"Clever."

"How restless men are to leave an everlasting mark. The source of their endless mythologizing and self-storytelling about their prowess and potential. And when those myths unravel, as they almost always do, men unravel along with them. By the time men are fifty-five, they spend most of their time recounting the stories they've told themselves and bitterly wondering how they were tricked into believing them at all. And yet, they will tell these stories to their sons, because without them men would have no orientation in the world at all."

"And women don't tell themselves such stories?"

"Of course they do; all humans do, but their orientation in the world does not depend upon it. Women's orientation in the world is more instinctive, an orientation they use endlessly to their advantage to shape the world around them. They can sense the smallest vibrations in human relations, because they sense the smallest vibrations in themselves, their awareness growing in concentric circles until so much is accounted for, but this awareness is also the source of their inexhaustible capacity to worry and complain. They are continuously in catfights because they know almost immediately what the other woman is up to while men remain retarded and trusting in their myths until reality crumbles them from within. This is part of the reason that sex is so important for men. It is their means of testing their mythical fitness for the world. But, of course, it is important for women too. As I said, once I discovered lovemaking with my Macedonian, I found the transposition I experienced on the steps of that church began to fade away along with my anxieties and neurosis. Though the trepidation I would once again find myself in that same place is still with me today, so haunting was it. Funny I should use the word 'haunting.' You see, as far as I could tell nothing triggered my breakdown, though years, many years later I would wonder if in fact something 'haunting' did. The month before, my mother and I had taken a weekend retreat to a small lake an hour or so from our home. She was a great bird watcher, and she was particularly enchanted by a little island on that lake where a hundred different types of birds thrived. We were there for the day and slept the night at a small hotel, and the next morning she said we would take a slight detour home because she wanted me to see something. It was a short drive, maybe forty kilometers, and honestly, it wasn't until we were right on it—maybe I was daydreaming as usual and not paying attention to the signs—I recognized it, Birkenau, from the pictures I saw at school. I knew about the terrible things that had happened there, and at the other concentration camps, of course, but I might as well have been living in America, say, for my contact with their physical reality. There are so many wounds crisscrossing Poland, so many. To not remember them would be a sin, but it would also be a sin to remember them too much."

"Near the end of Nietzsche's 'Use and Abuse of History,' he says something like history needs to be contained to not sap the power of youth, and its most 'beautiful privilege,' to grow in an atmosphere of innocence."

"And not just for the youth, but everyone, at every age, to a degree, no?"

"I think so."

"Yes, we must always provide it for ourselves. If we dwell too much on our past, especially on our sins . . . when we turn too far inward, we risk vanishing. Sometimes I wonder if we, I mean the educated class, the Hollywood class, all the liberal elites, we call them, have reached such a consciousness of this country's sins that we have an unconscious wish to destroy it."

"Is it more profitable that we remain ignorant?"

"It's better we admit how by the grace of God we exist at all. So, anyway, maybe this is why my mother waited until I was thirteen to take me to Birkenau, so different than Auschwitz I saw a year later. Auschwitz is like a museum, full of evidence of the atrocities, while Birkenau leaves the atrocities to your imagination. Some structures in ruins, fences and a watchtower at the top of the camp. Only the rail lines that ran into it and came to a sudden end sent shudders up my spine. I remember walking the length of it. There were only a handful of other people there, and it was gloomy that day, drizzling and gray. How eerie it felt."

"I imagine."

"I stole a broken brick, one of those used to

construct the ovens, and took it home as a memento. It is in my apartment, next to the knickknacks my father brought home to me. But, as I said, only many years later did I entertain the hypothesis that this visit had something to do with my collapse at the steps of St. Mary's. The intractability of evil in the human condition that, perhaps, I sensed was intractably planted in me as well."

I had music playing in the background, the Brandenburg Concertos, and now we quietly turned to it, listening with the attentiveness of toddlers at a magic show, neither of us saying a word for a few minutes.

"Thank you for having me," Sophia said. "If I hadn't found you, I don't know what would have become of me. I've burned so many bridges in my department."

We'd reached that well-earned place where what began as me stretching her had now turned into each of us stretching the other, like taffy on a taffy pull, creating the sweetest intimacy.

"And I value you too. Especially, I've noticed, your reluctance to embrace any theory, no matter how challenging, you can't honestly test against your experiences."

"Well, I've always felt I had no right to preach before I converted myself, or at least tried. What is the point of having all these brilliant theories and ideas if we don't allow them to turn us inside out? What is the point in them if we can't also spit them out?"

It was getting near 9:00 p.m. We'd been together from mid-morning, and she had a two-hour drive home. After determining for herself that she was sober for the road, she gathered her things. The question she posed to me was still there, still throbbing, though distinctly more weakly, as I walked her to her red Audi A6 and watched her drive away. I was happy to have dishes to wash and vaguely triumphant I comported myself precisely as the catechism commanded.

I felt relief, but not only from having put the predicament behind me. Now, alone, another thought was setting up in my head. Though she adored me and I adored her, little did she know how little I adored myself. If I drew close to her, I was afraid she'd see the sickalacrum I too had become, the entire self-satisfied gimmickry and increasing maliciousness of the so-called academic class I was a willing member of.

My thoughts now turned to that simple dick whose fate I was chosen to deliberate over, how within three weeks his identity had been outed and his mug featured full blown on placards with any number of accompanying slurs Sharpied over his head, turning the one-time piranha into an instant pariah. How did this small clumsy clod get an avalanche going? Butterfly effect, indeed, as one by one the complaints and accusations continued against dozens of other men, and the Greeks as a whole, until it reached such a pitch a newcomer to our greens might've concluded our fraternities were the most terrifying lions' dens where Caligulan debasements were being practiced with impunity (which, of course, they were, except the debased were the pledges). As for the performance artist/victim: She wasn't waiting for our review much less recommendation, and rather decided to get ahead of the curve, making an appearance on campus wearing a dress made of saturated red tampons, food coloring or real blood was anyone's guess. It was possible she'd parlayed a performance piece, still in its conceptual stage, into a fully realized work of art on this now national stage, a strange choice, I thought, as what she'd matter-of-factly stuck into herself monthly only had visual semblance to what had been stuck in her against her will and for that matter in the other hole. In any case, rape in hand, she'd finally found a meaning for her metaphor, to borrow from Gerty. It proved a moment of hysterical theatrical genius, tapping a nationwide nerve, and providing fantastic juice for the movement.

The tampon dress attracted a downtown gallery owner's attention, where, in his blog, he anointed it an instant, if minor, masterpiece, quieting and refining, as do all great works of art, a thousand different vectors of energy into a single fixed object. It inspired half a dozen other women to parade around campus wearing their own similes for sexual abuse. One woman set a menorah on her head with only the middle candle lit, obviously battery operated since nary did it sputter in the rain the day she sloshed across campus wearing it; an East-Asian woman sported a sari and had a bull's-eye instead of a third eye painted on her forehead, suggesting the innermost aspect of her spiritual life had become as exposed and vulnerable as a shooting-range target. To indicate the intolerable burden the patriarchy had foisted upon her womanhood, yet another was dragging around a huge Styrofoam ball and chain, except where there should've been one ball there were predictably two. It was a regular fashion show of the oppressed with the quad as the runway.

The dress got notice, but it wasn't until an unusually high-profile female singer, famous for her outlandish costumes, romped on stage wearing the bloody original (obviously pinned here and there as she was at least three sizes smaller), in a show of solidarity with the coed, asking that in the middle of her decadent and debauched spectacle tens of thousands pause for a somber moment of reflection for all those similarly wounded, that the whole affair went viral. *When Will He Stop*, the ballad she sang in observance, seemed apropos until one actually read the lyrics, as I did, whose refrain, "Stop so I can be gone of your love," had nothing to do with the coed's grievance. But by now, the irrationalities had turned into a kind of prerequisite for advancing the argument. I looked across the beautiful room at Shutters and recalled the hysteria that a serial date rapist was loose on campus whose identity the administration was protecting from fear of any number of reasons, the most preposterous that he was a family member of one of the higher-ups in the administration, or worse, one of the legacy kids, as they're called, scattered across the major.

Waving pink glow-in-the-dark wands, and toting on poles signage such as OUR BODIES R OURS, a several-hundred-strong army of students conducted a weeklong sunset vigil, starting at the Women's Studies office and wending their way to the provost's palace. A small contingent of English majors circulated a "sex compact"—as in agreement, hardly compressed and tidy—made up of twelve points, each to be initialed by the participants, and hand-cocked, I think it would be fair to characterize it as at this point, on the bottom, though not, mercifully, I suppose, notarized. If that weren't enough, a group of women's studies majors circulated a petition demanding an end to pornography, which under the guise of so-called "free speech" had been allowed to dangerously grow, they claimed. "We must now stand up and call pornography for what it is: Pornotution. Scopophiliacal sadism, female hyper-objectification. We call on campus administrators to immediately firewall against all pornotution web content, and censure those who still secure means to access it while on campus." Countless women were carrying a sign that read "1 in 5," numbers, I soon discovered, from one of my peers, which represented women who are raped on college campuses every year.

"It's a fact, according to a Department of Justice study; if you doubt me, I'll send it." This was offered by one of my colleagues, back at the review committee, where the pressure was building on me, and the consensus was that *The Red Dress* articulated to a T a certain critical wounded condition shared by women who up until that moment perhaps may not have been aware of their wounded condition, lying there in all its tattered and diabolical potential, at all, so when I asked the molested, "Why didn't you gather your clothes and walk out after you closed, say, Modigliani?" my colleagues made me to understand in no uncertain terms I needed to stand down.

"I was simply asking whether she had a choice over the matter when they were happily going at it."

"She was never 'happy' 'going at it.' She made clear she was uncomfortable from the start."

"When she was fondling herself in the mirror?"

"That was she in relation to her own body. It has nothing to do with what he did to her. Because a woman touches herself, doesn't mean she's inviting molestation."

"Then why didn't she leave from the start? He didn't grab her by the hair and drag her into his cave."

"Why don't women leave their husbands after they've been repeatedly battered. Why didn't the Jews leave Germany from the start?"

"Because they lived there? Because they had their synagogues, and family, and businesses rooted there for generations?"

"Haven't you ever heard of learned helplessness? You're mis-contextualizing. You do it frequently, I have to say, and it's getting problematic."

"There is a lot of self-righteousness going on here I find problematic. Did any of us consult THE MANUAL when we had our first go at sex? It's a messy business."

"You're full of all sorts of evasions, aren't you?" This from a historian from Flint whose father had worked on the auto assembly lines, the most interesting part of her rather extensive and tedious vitae.

"I'm sorry if all this isn't self-evident. But, the question should be: How do we educate our students to guard against things spiraling out of control?"

"Nothing spiraled out of control other than his own aggressiveness."

"So she had nothing to do with what happened?"

Historian: "As in, the victim is now responsible? That's an old trope. She invited the rape by dressing so scantily. I'm surprised to hear you saying this. I really am."

Another member of the committee, an anthropologist who studied the comings and goings of children at a zoo, now made me understand that even learned helplessness didn't adequately describe it; you see, under certain conditions women suffer under a kind of hypnotic of male energy, a fear of violent reprisal so deep-seated volition itself, as we commonly think of it, is vanquished. "There is definitely systemic sexism, but also what I might call 'psycho-structural sexism.'"

Enough, I guffawed.

I could feel their impatience with me growing. I'd become a serious obstacle, one that had to be surmounted, not because I was menacing, but because I was obstinate, and oblivious, as though I would forever be deaf to the river raging beneath the smooth table of ice upon which I, in my manhood, so casually skated.

My only open-minded ally was a tough dyke from our econ department who seemed so wholly man perhaps she'd passed to the dark side unannounced even to herself. "I think it's important we stay with our assignment," she said, "though these larger issues need airing as well." She too was incredulous that the woman had spent a good two hours with the guy and enjoyed a host of sexual favors before bolting from bed.

Regardless, fraternities were now required to conduct sensitivity programs for all their members, funded, I discovered, by the school's "healthy masculinity initiative," which aided "male-identifying students in programming around consent, rape culture, and healthy relationships." Two more safe spaces aside from the one we already had were thrown up, places where malevolent male energy might be exorcized and cookies, milk, a cuddle pillow, and a sympathetic ear made available.

When I brought the sex compact up for discussion in my undergraduate seminar on Chaucer, most of the students saw no harm in it, and, were, in fact, puzzled by the need to bring it up for debate at all. Their general take on the matter was if you aren't causing harm then what could possibly be the harm, and, if it is also true lawsuits in the thousands are pending over such an issue then why not protect the school against these. Is this why tuition has gone through the roof? Anyway, referring to their smart devices, they were used to the lack of privacy, if not inviting it, they wistfully admitted; their working assumption was that someone was snooping from somewhere at most anytime, but that was the price to pay for having a virtual valet at your instant disposal. Someone said a consent app was already on the market, so her only issue was, "Why waste paper?" Anyway, privacy implied you were hiding something, and hiding something implied there was something worth hiding and something worth hiding implied what you were hiding was embarrassing if not vaguely or outright criminal. Isn't it all about transparency? In any case, this wasn't about hiding anything, it was about agreement, consensus, mutual respect. Wasn't sex a kind of implicit contract? You treat me this way and I treat you that way, and whatever happens between us we agree will happen within our comfort levels? If I don't want to go there and you do, then with a written contract we can know this in advance. It isn't filed with some commission or anything; it was held between two people, so what's the big worry? How I wanted to tell them any sexual act worth its salt starts by way of resistance if not pain before it ascends to the summit of glory, but instead playing it safe, I said, "But do you want a certificate for every intimate encounter you have? What if someone you had sex with wants to someday use it against you, as a way to prove a point or collect some debts?" Huh? We went around and around, a few of the better students shaking their heads at why we were spending our time talking about this when "The Parson's Tale" was awaiting elucidation. Then it struck me that only one guy had thrown his opinion into the mix. "Guys, why are you all so mum?" There were a few hems and a couple of haws. I burst out in laughter at their reticence, barreling, apparently, across a line, as Samantha, one of the most negligible presences up until then in the class lurched from her seat mumbling/crying, “This isn’t a laughing matter.”

“It certainly isn’t. That’s the reason I’ve brought it up for discussion, but, from what is obvious, the guys have no interest in talking about it.”

“Maybe it’s time they listen instead. Also, twenty percent of women experience campus rape. The facts speak for themselves,” Dawn, one of my better students, said.

I asked, “Where do you get your numbers?”

Dawn: “It’s well known.”

“Facts are derived from studies, and, given that I’m on this committee, I took the time to read the study you’re referring to because, on the face of it, that’s a big number. A show of hands, how many of you are shocked twenty percent of the women on this campus have been raped?”

Nearly all the men and a quarter of the women.

I said, “So, let’s look at the study. It surveyed around six thousand students, from two universities, and was about sexual assault in general, which meant anything from unwanted contact to forced rape.”

“Unwanted contact means what?” someone asked.

“A kiss on the cheek that wasn’t welcome. A

pat on the back. Of the twenty percent, around half that number of students were actually raped, rape defined as nonconsensual sex, above and beyond unwelcome physical contact."

Samantha: "You're saying ten percent are raped, then?"

"The study is saying that. Well, let's go further into the study, and see what rape looked like on these college campuses."

Samantha: "What do you mean, 'what it looks like'?"

"What the study has to say about who is a victim, when and how and under what circumstances it occurs."

"Go ahead," Chandra, a lesbian poetess, said.

"I wasn't waiting for your okay. This is a pretty important matter that deserves careful consideration, because not only are women vulnerable but men are too. Vulnerable not only because they also get raped, almost always by another man, but because at any moment if they aren't more careful and chivalrous, then they might find themselves pegged as rapists too."

Chandra: "Chivalry? Watch your hems while stepping over the puddle, ladies."

I chuckled, and said, "Chivalry is a word that conjures all sorts of stereotypical images, you're right, but, in truth, it's a decent enough guiding philosophy of how men should treat women: with respect and dignity."

Chandra: "Lest our fragile selves break! How about equality?"

"Note, by the way, how deferential for the most part you are to what I might have to say about Chaucer's tales, but when it comes to these matters, suddenly my intention has been compromised, because, I have to assume, I'm a man."

"Or the patriarchal stereotype you're living up to," Dawn said.

"Well, let's take a look at the typical victim which the study gives us a good picture of. She was either a freshman or a sophomore, more likely than not to belong to a sorority. At a Friday or Saturday night frat party, she started drinking and hooked up with some guy she liked and trusted, so much so somewhere between midnight and the wee morning hours they stumbled to either his place or hers, and start fooling around. Sound familiar?"

There was some twittering, the actual and the other kind, I suspected.

"According to the study, she liked having sex and liked to get drunk before having it, but in this instance she was so drunk she more or less passed out on the bed, at which point she obviously couldn't consent to anything of a physical nature, so whatever happened afterward was considered rape. When she woke, she was highly unlikely to have sustained any kind of physical injury and almost zero chance of sustaining an injury involving a weapon like a knife or gun, but emotionally she felt traumatized."

"Who wouldn't?" said Samantha. "Think about it; waking up and finding out something's been done to you against your will. The psychic scars it would leave. So dehumanizing."

I nodded my head in agreement and continued, "The study also looked deeper into the victim's past. As it turned out, she had a history of sleeping around and dating guys whom she characterized as physically or verbally abusive. And it wasn't the first time something like this had happened to her, in fact, she was eight times more likely than her peers, who never encountered such a thing, to have experienced sexual assault before coming to college."

Dawn: "That's natural. She'd been traumatized by some guy when she was younger and kept repeating the trauma in the hopes of working it out psychologically."

Samantha: "Did it look at the guy? I bet he was eight hundred times more likely to have done this kind of thing before coming to college."

"No, the study didn't, but that might make for a good follow-up study."

Dawn: "So what's your point?"

"At this point, I'm not making a point at all, only letting you know what the study you were referring to found."

Samantha: "According to your reading of it! I'm not sure how, as a man, you're qualified to read this study. It seems to me you're not reading it, but interpreting it, to promote the same old dehumanizing line: The girl who got raped got raped because she was loose and drunk."

"If you have any doubt that what I'm reporting isn't in the study, of course, I'll be happy to provide you all with a link to it so you can read it for yourself. Lastly, the study looks at what the girl did in response to the rape. Not much is the answer. She talked to a friend or family member about it, but regarding going to the police or the school officials, she didn't bother."

"Sure, she was humiliated, shamed, afraid to make what happened to her public. What's so surprising about that?" Samantha said.

"I'm not saying it's surprising. But, do you think if she were robbed in a car at gunpoint she would have reported it?"

Dawn: "Sex is different. It goes to your identity."

"Well, the reason she didn't report it is she didn't think it was a big enough deal to report. She didn't report it, file charges, or seek a restraining order, but instead, dealt with it by avoiding the rapist from there on out."

Actually, I didn't finish saying that before Samantha stomped out of the room, after which Dawn stood all protective, like a nanny whose charge had been cuffed by a stranger, and ran after her, and then Chandra threw up her arms and hollered, "You just don't get it. Sexist!" And left too.

She was a poet, as I said, who wrote prose (and probably poetry) poorly and already we'd had two discussions about her bad habit of crossing from one thought to the other without the ricketiest of bridges, a writing technique, she claimed, meant to convey the "discontinuity of knowledge" and "uncanniness of simultaneities," which might've sufficed for explanation in one of those so-called creative nonfiction classes but crashed on its ass for writing cogently about Chaucer. She led a writers group on campus, where, according to her flier, "cisgender women, nonbinaries, transgender and gender nonconforming women" were welcome, meaning any combination of any orientation, however far-flung, except straight men. Twice, I noticed, we'd hopped into our respective cars in the same parking garage, about ten minutes away by foot, so one rain-pounding evening I suggested we go together, as I noticed she hadn't an umbrella when she stepped outside. She accepted the offer, and we small-talked, our shoulders touching now and again until we reached the garage, where I collapsed the umbrella and asked about her arms, which she'd been scratching furiously. "I burned it bad," she said and drew her sleeve back. A bruise variegated like the Milky Way extended the length of her forearm. She explained, "A couple of weeks ago I spilled a cup of boiling water on it." I took her arm in the cup of my hand, a simple act, but like a rubber band, she snapped it back, what I took to be a flinch from pain before she made clear that "that was inappropriate. So was the way you nudged up against me when we were walking here." A few rejoinders flew through my brain, but I decided to leave without a word. I didn't for the life of me see there was a fuse between us that could be lit with a few innocent shoulder bumps, but, there it was, boom! Who was capable of navigating such a hyper-sensitive world? Who'd lowered the bar of offense to this dehumanizing height, so that you had to be practiced in limbo from birth to squeeze beneath it? This was a virtual return of the Puritans. The era of "It." "It" is their fear and loathing of the masculine; the vigilance demanded of them in every quarter and at every corner to keep it from overwhelming; their utter exhaustion at having to incessantly monitor all the unspoken male aggression, the near dark matter of it, that was so commonplace, so much part of men's inherited station and congenital makeup that even their most mind-splitting and solemn introspection proved useless in rooting it out. "It" was beyond argument, if argument itself was nothing more than a ruse for those in positions of privilege to redirect if not derail the juggernaut of historical reality they were now using to batter your age-old castle to smithereens. "No matter how hazy and labyrinthine our logic might look to you," they were near to confessing, "from our perspective it is obvious and orthogonal as a cattle car headed for Treblinka. Our reason needs no REASON, because what we are ultimately speaking of here is a mystical level of suffering so black and complete that the light of language cannot pierce it. Perhaps only storytelling, where facts and fiction kiss, is an adequate medium for expressing our reality."

I was sure some sophomoric version of this was passing through the brains of the guys in the room because they went almost instantly and univocally from reserved to dumb, sunken in like children interpolating at the speed of light what all this meant for them, including the orphanage, as mom starts slinging dishes. As it was happening, I was doing some pretty swift interpolating myself: Should I press on in spite of the twisted face ten yards away from my own; what is my duty in such circumstances; do I compromise the fabric of my person and profession by backing off and letting this hydra hold court; do I vacate the ground that makes this place sacred; would I throw gas on their ire by keeping my composure? Was there a way to turn this into a so-called learning experience? "You're sexist!" She might have been a card-carrying member of the Cheka throwing roses at the feet of Lenin as he ascended the steps of the Kremlin, ushering in a new kind of red terror. I'd seen it gathering on the horizon, a tsunami that had taken decades to form, and suddenly there it was, and there I was, precisely as they calculated, shouting from the tumult only to find water getting sucked into my lungs.

Two days later, the emails started showing up, making me think how stupid I was to inform my class I was on the committee and how apparently eager my students were to spread the information to their most zealous peers. They were delivered to my inbox into the wee morning hours, 2:10 and 3:24 a.m., for actual examples, making me wonder why these petitioners weren't asleep, studying, or, frankly, fucking their lights out rather than neuroticizing over a case that remained complicated, even for me, even though I'd spent a good month studying it down to the most cataract-inducing details. One after another attempted to sway me, and in only one direction, to sentence the Lothario to death, the opening of their epistle invariably respectful, then growing homiletic, and finally shrill. Then an email with the subject line "Watching" hit my inbox. "We are waiting and watching, but in the end, we will not let our voices be silenced and let injustice win the day. Who do you think YOU are? Why don't YOU just get up and walk out?"

Some were waiting, and others were not. A week after the emails started pouring in, I was tooling around town in my vintage VW van when I noticed the foulest smell coming out of nowhere. I thought it was wafting in from the outside, but when I rolled the windows up within a minute the stench was drilling up into my nose. Had a spare burrito or something dropped beneath the seat? I found a few crumbs is all, so I took the van to the carwash for deluxe interior cleaning, only to discover when I was back on the road that the smell had gotten unbelievably, intolerably worse. I'd had enough and headed to the auto shop and told my mechanic to root it out, at any cost, as I was now near vomiting after traveling more than five miles. Within minutes he pulled from a crevice between the manifold and the crankshaft a small, half-decomposed roasting bird. "Did a pigeon try to set a nest there?" I actually asked my mechanic, before it dawned on me someone had popped the hood of my van and jammed this fowl in there; this was a schoolboy version of the horsehead in the bed.

Driving away with the evidence sealed tight in a gallon-size pickle jar, the militant nature of the movement I was an impediment to blood-chillingly struck me. In spite of the emails, I suppose a small part of me still believed this could be worked out through give and take, an academic dialogue, however contentious, while all along more like a manifesto had been drawn up that brooked no critique. Anything was possible now. I began parting blinds and turning my peripheral vision into a fixed part of my consciousness. I contacted the assistant dean and set up a meeting, at which point he answered he meant to contact me for a meeting as well, so the timing was perfect, indeed. Maybe he'd been cc'd on the threatening emails? In the meantime, I kept a diary of my daily comings and goings so my loved ones and the law would have some idea of my whereabouts and routines in case I came up missing. A couple of hours before that meeting, it dawned on me that the email I received with the rhetorical question, "Why don't you just get up and walk out?" wasn't so rhetorical after all, as it mirrored the very question I asked the rape victim during our interview: "Why didn't you just get up and walk out?" It was an inside job! One of my so-called colleagues or the victim herself was behind the threats! Carrying my notes, diary, and, naturally, the bird in the bottle (in a plastic shopping bag), I rushed into the AD's office and took a seat, only to have him convey, before I could submit my evidence, that a student had filed a complaint of sexual harassment against me, and, as a matter of protocol, they now had to follow up.

"Sexual harassment? Ridiculous."

"The accusation of sexual harassment is always serious."

"True enough, the reason the accusation shouldn't be leveled because a prof once took a sneak peek at a girl's cleavage, for instance."

I watched him pick up a pen and scribble something on a notepad. An MBA with an emphasis on so-called Human Resources, he was one of those bureaucratic sycophants hired to monitor, sideline, silence, and occasionally eliminate those who stood in the way of the school's destiny.

"Who lodged this accusation? Let me guess," I said.

"Chandra Silver in your Chaucer class."

"What I thought. This must be comeuppance from a whopper of a fight we had last week."

"A fight?"

"It turned into one."

"Was there a physical alter—"

"She lost her wits and accused me of being sexist. She and two other students claimed I didn't 'get it' after I brought up a research study for discussion. In any case, I reached out to all of them the day after, to talk it through, but never heard back. They kept coming to class, and I thought the whole thing had blown over. Apparently not."

"You said they said you didn't get it. What is it?"

"That's the hundred-dollar question, isn't it?"

"These are sensitive times."

"Too."

"I'm not sure we can ever be sensitive enough."

"It's obvious the evidence points in the opposite direction; too much sensitivity and you break out in a rash."

He narrowed his eyes, in worry or anger I couldn't say.

"These days, if you don't like fried chicken and waffles, you're one step from lynchin' a black man. A passerby who hands a donut to a homeless guy is a communist sympathizer." I laughed, to myself, naturally.

"I'm not sure why this is funny."

"It's hysterical, actually. Look at the joke you people have made of the English language alone: alterity, subaltern, not to mention intersectionality, scopophilia, heteronormativity, and, naturally, diversity. Forget about a rash: You've got us gasping from anaphylaxis. Oh, I almost forgot about the male gaze!" I widened my eyes and put up two fingers like pincers for effect.

"Perhaps these are concepts you need to embrace rather than deride."

"Has it ever occurred to you not a single poet we study would be caught dead using these distortions? Anyway, I've had my hands full with hope, faith, and love. Do those words offend you, Deanlet? Should I say oops?"

"Deanlet? Are you attempting to insult me?"

"What are the specifics of her gripe against me, this Chandra girl?"

"That you walked her to her car one evening

and made a pass at her."

"I walked her to her car, true. But the pass part is bullshit."

"That you touched her inappropriately as well."

"And how does your field manual define 'inappropriately'?"

"I'm sure this is perfectly clear to you already, but in case, for whatever reason, it isn't, the answer is any way the victim defines it. Sexual harassment can be interpreted from an inappropriate look."

How had these ideas slithered beneath your bed as you snoozed, like a bloody python, wrapping up your every ridiculous limb?

"It's concerning to some that you continue to assume gender pronouns when addressing students."

"It takes some getting used to: ze, zirs, zig, zag."

"It's not complicated, actually. A simple question—"

"—that has to be asked every time you address someone, because a person can change gender at the drop of a hat. Check in regularly, exclamation mark, your website advises us."

"At a minimum, we'd like you to attend a sensitivity training workshop."

How ironical, I thought, the most resolutely irreligious were now schooling us like the grimmest eighteenth-century nuns.

"But funny you should call me in," I said, "because I've been getting a number of threatening emails. Maybe from Chandra Silver. And this."

I lifted the pickle jar from my bag and put it on his desk.

"What is that?"

"I think a Cornish game hen, though it might be a chicken. It's hard to say exactly, what with all the decay."

"What is it doing here? In that jar?"

"Well, I wanted you to see it for yourself."

"Please take it off my desk. Are you mad?"

I explained it all to him with surprising relish, down to the enormous tongs the mechanic used to pry it from the crevice.

"This is a fairly grave issue. Serious."

With that, he asked bureaucratically whether I felt the need for campus police protection, his gray-blue eyes falling rather tactlessly to the side to read some document clearly more important than the conversation, or me.

"This brings us to a larger point," he said. "We've been trying to shape the curricula to reflect concerns closer to the students' interest, you've undoubtedly noticed. The jar, please."

"I should think you'd be used to putrefaction. But to your point about the curricula: It's always a good idea to keep things fresh."

"Enrollment in your undergraduate classes has shrunk considerably, over, say, the last five years?"

"People aren't as interested in Shakespeare and Chaucer as they used to be, if you haven't noticed."

"We've been discussing letting Liona Hart teach Shakespeare."

"You mean the one with the course on vampires in literature and film?"

"She's well trained in Shakespeare, as you must know."

"Terrible idea."

"We can disagree without being disagreeable. Let's leave it there. You're still grading on a curve."

"So."

"A curve does not fit the diverse profile of the students we have today. We've had numerous complaints about grading that some have suggested reflects a certain bias against certain identity groups of students."

He finally mustered the courage to reach for the jar. But in a deliberately unhinged way, I yelled, "Don't tamper with the evidence," and scooted the fowl closer.

He put his hands up in a gesture of surrender, cleared his voice, and said, "Of course, you have and will always have full authority to grade as you see fit."

"Should I be relieved?"

"I think you should consider the broader charter of the school toward diversity and inclusiveness."

"I'm a teacher, not a social engineer. And some of my best students are so-called people of color, just in case you're curious. They don't need your 'broader charter.'"

"So-called?"

"What is your function, really? Is it a coincidence once people like you came on board the madness took root? Is your greatest nightmare that faculty will take over and return us to the dark days of learning?"

"We might be willing to work with you in a way that would suit you, and us."

"Let me teach the way I want. Stay out of my hair."

"Toward an early retirement. Some package that might work for you."

I did a quarter turn of the jar and pretended to ponder it for a beat.

"Is the dean in on this discussion? I'm nowhere near retirement."

“The dean and the provost.”

“Provost. Did you know the word originated in the eleventh-century? And it was used to designate the keeper of the prison?”

“Are you happy here?” he asked in a tired and sad voice, as if wondering whether I had considered hospice.

“What gives you the impression I’m not, and, frankly, do you care?”

“You are part of a community, and when that community senses your unhappiness, and, let’s be honest here, your hostility, then the community suffers.”

“Your description better describes a cult than a college. Anyway, I’ve kept my nose out of everyone’s business.”

“You don’t hide your grievances nearly as well as you imagine. The school is moving in a direction you are clearly not comfortable with.”

“Self-destructive?”

“The fact is, we have students applying here in record numbers.”

“And accruing record debt. What do you people do with all that money anyhow?”

“And we’re now in the top twenty in the country.”

“In no small part due to teachers like me.”

"You have a good fifteen years and more before retirement. That's a long time to feel so alienated from this community. Might Ms. Silver's outburst be a reflection of that feeling? Students expect a different relationship with their teachers. It's more of a conversation between their expectations and yours, and we feel this reality is becoming more and more uncomfortable for you."

"What the hell are you talking about, honestly?"

"You've had a close relationship with many of your students over the years."

"True."

"Inviting them out."

"Do we need to fill out a form to grab a cup of coffee?"

"To your home?"

"When I was down for a month, last year, I did my classes at home, yes. I had serious surgery on my knee; maybe your informant didn't mention it. With that said, I confess—funny I should use that word, huh? I confess I may have been remiss for not providing crumpets and tea."

"At one time, you were quite active on Facebook."

"Until hair transplant ads started popping up on my home page."

“You have several students, past and present, as Facebook friends. A series of IM exchanges with a certain student has raised some concerns.”

“A certain student?”

“I’m not at liberty to disclose who made the complaint.”

“Then the nameless complainant can kiss my nameless ass.”

“I think we can wrap this up at this time.”

“Naturally, one must keep the dossier open, *gehe ich recht*, Herr Miller?”

“Pardon me?”

“Has it ever occurred to you that the Gestapo is saving *you* for dessert?”

Boiling, I left. But it didn’t last long. I now recalled how minutes after exiting the inquisitor’s chamber, the *auto-da-fé* commenced; how I sifted and sorted through my conscience looking for any evidence that I might have crossed a line. For instance, had I gone too far in criticizing a student, male or female, ze or zer, suggesting they put a little more heft into a paper; or smiled too long at a certain mixed-race student in my Spenser course whose bouncy locks of golden brown hair hung sexily down to her even sexier bum; or asked any number of them to put their smart devices down long enough to focus on the question I put in front of them? I wondered if I should've refrained from using certain words, like "lazy," or "banal," or "lovely," this in connection to a coed's concluding remarks for an essay she'd written on "The Summoner's Tale." Now comments like "I would suggest next time you make such an assertion you check in with your brain" seemed gratuitously mean. If that weren't enough, even your most sympathetic observer would've surely concluded that your attempt to undermine the orthodoxy surrounding campus rape culture with a pointed synopsis of the 1-in-5 study was all but empty of empathy. Yes, the study showed what it showed, but did this mean you had to shove it so mercilessly down students' throats? Let's face it: You'd been outed. You intended your criticisms to cut to the bone and believed your professorial status and tenure would shield you from retaliation. Now, a little licking of the AD's ass and perhaps a follow-up letter of repentance along with a few choice words for your students, in the vein of "I'm sorry; my insensitivity has hurt many of your feelings," would clear the stench from the room and get your academic life, such as it was, back on track, and pave the way for a smooth retirement, not the shatteringly degrading one they'd cobbled together for your consideration.

As I tramped back across the low-carbon-footprint campus, through the small sustainable gardens and past the water-efficient fountains, and between rows of drip-line-fed trees that ended at the steps of green-energy buildings and their stone facades inscribed with verities like "the most difficult thing in life is to know yourself," ostracism, it dawned on me, was the worst sort of punishment, a kind of living death. This was my home; my life and way of being in the world. How I suddenly found myself in a position I frankly never believed was possible, in a place like this, and this place in particular, where I spent twenty years giving my all, was mindboggling, very near the feeling of being betrayed by a lover, where what you believed was the case turned out to be the opposite, where what you thought you'd built piece by piece was upended piece by unbelievable piece.

Yes, I might just as well have been served divorce papers by some stone-faced courier. Indeed, I was reliving the shocking nausea of my actual divorce all over again. Reliving how my wife's eyes, so attentive for so long, had turned to daggers, and how using the cord that once bound us together we fashioned our cruelest garrots. How from a few motley parts floating about in my brain she engineered me into an elaborate and preposterously efficient war machine and then took the bitterest measures to combat it until she was in effect waging the most outlandish war against her own imaginings, which far from weakening or killing her off made her more kinetic and formidable. Eventually, my protests proved so unprofitable I was reduced to muteness and the blankest stares, which aggravated her more than my hollering. For two years it went on this way, staying as far as possible away from the truth, even my tiny version of it, in fear of saying anything that might light the fuse, or rather fuses, hidden everywhere, mostly invisible, and ignited by the remotest flame. Everything that was, as it turned out, was not, like the blackest magic trick had been played on you without you knowing the magician was present, until love, and love itself, seemed the cruelest ruse of them all; bickering for a full month over a gift I'd given her, which was either hers to keep or part of our community property. Over a few thousand dollars of books and bikes and a barbeque, these stupid little stand-ins for our proxy war over who hurt who the most. What pathos! What a humiliation to watch yourself turn into everything you most detested until finally you cry uncle to get out from beneath the barbed monstrosity you'd become. Would this be my most unendurable fate going forward if I chose to stay in the academy? Would I battle this miserableness now on an institutional scale?

In the middle of all this, I was called on by the son of a former girlfriend, a French geographer with whom I had a whirlwind romance for a month or so in Paris during a sabbatical leave, until we both realized, at more or less the same time, that neither of us was suited for the other. Still, no need to be American about it, we fucked on and off until I left, and stayed close friends, close enough so that I helped steer her son, Philippe, to our school for study (engineering) and met up with him every few weeks to keep track of his progress. He was a vaguely self-destructive genius, haughty and handsome, all of which got him laid with enviable regularity, and so my hunch was that he wanted to gather intel on how to navigate in this suddenly pharisaical environment. Sure enough, when we met, first up on the menu was the tampon dress. "*Incroyable*," he said, how shameless and tasteless Americans are; in Paris, she'd be driven off campus if only because she'd managed her complaint so crudely. I told him I wasn't so sure, that catcalling had been made a fineable offense in France, and, as for here, he needed to monitor his lubricious behavior closely. I told him I was on the committee looking into the recent rape case, and about the threatening emails I'd received, and the dean's dissecting of my every motivation and move. "Any idea who might be behind the emails?" he asked. "Could be anybody," I said, but more than likely it was an inside job, possibly perpetrated by the Deanlet himself. Philippe could easily tell the approximate location of the email's source by tracking the IP number, so when I got home I forwarded the emails to him, and three days later he called with news that the IP numbers were tracking through the school server. I asked if he could hone in any better; this would require hacking the server, not in his wheelhouse, but smack in the middle of one of his friend's, a hacktivist who'd been plying his trade since he was old enough to trike through the streets of Beijing. Excellent. I began to feel the criminal's sense of restless exhilaration, a maniacal righteousness at the prospect of slicing through the scummy veil right into the fleshy underbelly of the perpetrator, starting with my new arch enemy. Inside of a week, I had a thumb drive of the Deanlet's emails in hand.

What did this man actually do? Funneling a few dollars here and a few dollars there, working the most forgettable workshops and training sessions, recruiting for jobs whose titles were so contorted you'd think they were conjured for a laugh; overseeing countless half-wits in half a dozen departments to worry over problems a generation ago might've been tidied up by a few faculty members over a glass of wine. Good lord, if I didn't loathe him so profoundly I might very well have pitied him. And then I came upon a short exchange with the parents of the performance artist who, touché, were donors to the art department. Though they didn't precisely frame their concern for justice as a quid pro quo, there was no way to avoid the threat that if our committee didn't conclude what they wanted us to conclude, what they'd pledged to the department (a measly ten thousand bucks over three years, I discovered) would be diminished if not disappeared.

Now, I belatedly concluded, what to do with this smoking gun short of admitting I was part of a criminal network? Yes, after the thrill was gone, as they say, this smoking gun still had several rounds in its chamber, and all on its own had pivoted toward my head. How could I be sure the Chinese boy wouldn't be tracked down and confess? How about the way out of nowhere my screen in a nanosecond went blank and then just as suddenly refreshed? What a wretched penned-up creature the academy had turned me into, without any street instinct that might serve me in the face of such far-fetched threats. That man who looked at me a little too long? The student who tarried after class and turned something, hidden camera or mic, in her backpack off? Or the random parked car down the block where the guy in a black suit watched me for far longer than normal? Normal itself, the atmosphere through which we unconsciously drift, was now a dangerous maze over which snipers focused their scopes.

A small and boisterous meet-up of men shook me out of these recollections. There were six of them, sharply dressed and groomed down to the last blade of hair, sharing hugs and kisses and the most dramatic compliments, before settling into an ensemble of couches and armchairs in front of the fireplace, reserved for them, apparently, since it had been empty until now as others were elbowing for a seat at the bar. What cutting-edge subculture gays enjoyed only twenty years earlier, I thought, taking a sip of my martini, with their mesmerizing tales, tall or not, of sweaty sex clubs, brimming with rimming. We could always count on them to lead the way to every manner of joyful depravity, but how contented they now looked, having all but forfeited the juiciest of rendezvous with their chickens and hawks, dandelion-tender twinks, and gorilla-size studs, all that coconut-oiled buggering for some Guatemalan nanny to pamper their adopted Croatian kid, or that West Elm sofa for their cozy Los Feliz home. Sex was their primal therapy, their psychic balm and collective calm, and it cost them little more than the price of a drink, if that. Sure, they had the blistering reality and stinking stigmata of AIDS to bear, but nothing, in simple retrospect, a stash of condoms couldn't remedy until they found a cure. Shame dragged them from their dazzling nooks into the dullest mid-century-modern-inspired family lives.

One of the men, wearing a bright red jacket, now stood and like a contortionist extended his arms in a locked position behind his neck and blonde hair, bringing to mind those red Christmas flowers with a long spadix, anthurium, I think they're called. Yes, they got their equality only to find themselves a barely contained shambles shuttling about town with a yappy dog and a toddler strapped down in an eco-friendly car. How snugly they now fit into this sludge, this self-congratulatory and go-nowhere hellhole of a city, if not the self-congratulatory go-nowhere hellhole of existence itself. Everyone is looking for the most efficient means to arrive at the place of acceptability and respectability, only to arrive at a place where they can be drugged and then clubbed to death, I thought. They struggle and plead to come in from the margins only to find the center is the very place where you get to be tire-ironed into obedience, if not oblivion. The gays understood it all. Out there, at the margins, they realized the farce at the heart of civilization, if not at the heart of the human condition, and one of their perennial talents was making a farce of the farce. "There is an endless font of injury and revenge inside of each person," Sophia wrote, "but these are the shuddering reflection of the violations we all suffer, suffer as a matter of civilization per se, and the more civilization we enjoy, the more we suffer from it. The reason neurosis grows in proportion to sophistication" (from *Decadence and Farce from Warhol to Koons*).

Look at Santa Monica, I thought: a city polished to the point of nausea, like some super-sized Jeff Koons project, a place where nearly every aspect of life and nearly every life form is scrutinized for the most infinitesimal microbe that might in the least upset the delicate chemical balance of the hysterical acolytes that call this place home; a place patrolled by an endless number of jackboots enforcing an endless number of codes and ordinances, there to string you up for so much as inhaling the wrong way. Sure, it is teeming with sensuality, to the point of tedium, actually, but what of it when bureaucratic sadists whose ultimate goal is to disarticulate every aspect of the human situation that does not comport with their outlandish agenda control the show. Yes, what used to be the Puritans' purview has now become the purview of paranoid gender-neutral emotionally anxious bureaucrats. It is almost axiomatic that those who most want to control others end up drafting the laws, hence, what rules they ultimately arrive at, after deliberating with their personal psychoses, are in their personal interest, not the common interest in the least, if not utterly averse to the common interest, much less human interest. Yes, where for most of human civilization people lived near or visited the ocean to take advantage of its surfeit of exotica, tantalizing spices and fabrics and flesh, today they come here to live in a kind of willed anemia, a kind of paranoid Buddhism, where everything meaty, sweet, or rich has been jettisoned for food fit for ruminants, weeds and tubers, every off-putting sub-staple the human situation has struggled with the greatest effort to eradicate from its diet since it stood on two feet. Yes, the most satisfying food, as humans have come to indulge in it for hundreds of years, has been forfeited here for feasting on the abstract idea of life itself, turning our national immune system so weak that we break out in hives watching a wasp weave. Making us susceptible to the most tedious and tendentious remedies, like "listening as if it mattered," or "tuning into the secret within," or the sophomoric "master classes" of a TV personality, or all those ridiculous Tedx talks, or, worst of all, practicing "empathy," a word, if there ever was one, that broke the boner's back. How had our deepest psychological discoveries gotten substituted for the shallowest mantras of social workers? Don't they understand the rapist haunting their dreams is foremost the rapist of time itself, the dismembering clock ticking mercilessly inside of us; the only predictable and precise mechanism in the waste of our bodies, the thick and simmering stew that we are?

"Everywhere I turn, I see abandoned bodies," Sophia told me one afternoon at a park a few blocks from the school. I remember she had brought a large and amazingly colorful blanket for us to sit on, which she unfolded square by square until it proved big enough for a pow wow.

"Are we expecting others?" I asked.

She smiled and folded her legs, full lotus, taking in the sun and air.

"Flexible," I said. "But what do you mean by abandoned bodies?"

"I suppose the fear of touching or being touched. The unyoking that is going on. It must go hand in hand with our masturbatory culture, the masturbatory nature of so much human inquiry and discovery these days. From the endless germs we fear, to the libraries we avoid, to the porn sites we visit. Are we sanitizing our humanity into a kind of extinction? I suppose it is a feeling those who practice yoga, which means yoked, can sense better than most. But I should say practiced, because I haven't studied seriously in years. I started, believe it or not, in Poland."

"Yoga in Poland. That must've been a sight."

"An American girl who moved there with her boyfriend a few years after the wall fell, she was my first teacher. Back then, the streets were full of guitar-playing, Gauloises-smoking twenty-year-olds. They thought they were the new Lost Generation but mostly turned out to be the same old drunken one."

"Nice."

"A documentarian, from Chicago, I took as a boyfriend for about a year. My parents were appalled by his long beard and dreadlocks, but I found him handsome and fascinating: We used to sit in our main square where he'd film the passers-by, old men noisily blowing their noses, grandmas carrying homemade snacks wrapped in handkerchiefs, alcoholics ranting about who knows what. 'Why are you wasting your time on all this?' I asked him. He told me his theory of film was to film everything, every single detail, indeed, the single details per se, what he called the quotidian is what would one day tell THE STORY of how Poland had faired in the crumbled wall's wake."

"I imagine there was an amazing outpouring of artistic and creative production then."

She nodded, but then said, "Not necessarily. We would hear older poets and writers, and even some painters, complain: Under communism at least they had an evil to resist. A banner to gather under. Under capitalism, everybody was doing his own thing and forced to create in a kind of vacuum. There is value in an enemy, no? Why we keep them coming, as they say. Our triumphs over them give us direction and purpose."

"Humans abhor a vacuum the same way nature does."

"I look around at the nature of most of America's protesting and think what else can explain this outrageousness if not the need to fill a vacuum, to issue a protest to offset the hideous hollowness of our human condition. This hideous hollowness our greatest poets are able to turn into hymns."

"So there is no way to avoid this vacuum, you think."

"God can fill it, of course. His creation of us, his love and grace."

"Isn't all that just another story we tell ourselves?"

"You remind me of Johan a little."

"Not sure, yet, if that's a compliment."

She smiled and said, "Once we were at the main square, sitting on the steps that lead up to the statue of our national poet, Adam Mickiewicz. You know him?"

"I'm afraid I don't."

"I will give a few poems to you next week. Anyway, we were sitting on the steps when an old man with a cane began chiding us. What had we done that he should be so angry with us all the sudden? The gentleman walked up jabbing his cane and answered, 'Kissed!' How dare we sit in the shadow of such a great voice and act so disrespectfully. Johan apologized, which softened the man up, so much so that he began to tell of how Mickiewicz had saved him when he was young, and right there this old man recited one of Mickiewicz's most important poems, about two friends, one who visits the other after he'd been released from Siberia, only to find him an empty shell:

I'd learn the truth,
The truth that tyrants hide, the Polish truth.
It flourishes in shadows. Its history
Lives in Siberia where its heroes die,
There and in dungeons. But what did my friend
say?
He said he had forgotten. And, with dismay,
I listened to his silence. His memory was
Written upon, and deeply, but, because
It had long rotted in the dark, my friend
Could not read what was written: 'We'd
better send
For God. He will remember and tell us all.'

"After the man left, Johan said, 'It is sad only God, who is obviously dead, can remember what we've been through.' This irritated me. 'You find everything interesting. Why is it only God is the exception?' I said this quite innocently, but my own words would echo inside of me for many years to come."

"And you followed Johan to America?"

She gently slapped my wrist. "I will tell you about that. Be patient, Professor. Have you ever watched a child as a story unfolds, present at every step and only barely guessing what will happen next, versus the learned and intelligent types who jump so far ahead they forfeit the joy of discovery?

So, one evening a group of friends, ten of us, bought some weed and at Johan's tiny apartment we put on some music and lit some candles and began talking of what, after graduation, we hoped to do and achieve. It was an important discussion, so Johan fixed his camera on us, so that in ten, twenty years we might all look back and see where we'd arrived in respect to where we hoped we'd arrive."

"And your hope?"

"Very vague, only I knew it involved some great and impractical adventures. Anyway, we talked and smoked and drank our vodka until well after midnight when our friends left. Back on the couch, Johan and I began making out. We were about to slip out of our clothes when I remembered the camera. 'Let it run,' he said. I protested, but secretly I found the idea thrilling: tomorrow we could double our thrill by making love while watching ourselves make love. But when we played it back, the next day, the reality of it did not live up to the idea. Blah! This must have been, oh, mid-February, and a couple of months later was graduation, the day we all disappeared into Carnival when the streets are given over to the students, and Krakow turns into a bacchanalian free-for-all. I honestly lost track of time, and when

I stumbled home, finally, I found my parents waiting for me, with terrible looks on their faces. Had they heard gossip of my craziness, maybe normal for my peers, but beyond the pale for a diplomat's daughter? If only it was all so innocent." Sophia paused, and sadly shook her head. "No, my father said a video had been brought to his attention by a staff member, and he believed there might be a copy in circulation."

"Don't say it."

"'A video of you and that American. Being intimate,' he said. He could barely look at me, and immediately I knew to get out of this predicament would take great artistry. I swallowed my panicked heart and told him something completely within the realm of possibility: 'Someone has it out for you. Have your enemy bring you the so-called sex tape.' I went on and on, denying it with all my might, enumerating his possible antagonists; there was no shortage of them. I prayed that the American had only mentioned it to a friend who had gossiped it up. Our only phone was in the living room, and I didn't dare call him, so I rushed to his flat. He explained that one of our friends wanted a copy of the tape of our conversation and so the last time he was in Warsaw he'd taken the original to a video shop he'd used on a regular basis and told them to copy only the first hour, two hours short of when our sex tape began. He played the copy to make sure nothing compromising was on it before he handed it over to our friend. Some eavesdropper, you call them, at the video shop had either viewed the sex part and spread the word, or had made a copy, or multiples, and passed it around. Today, in America, this sounds terrible but hardly calamitous, but remember, this was Poland, the most Catholic of all the European countries and absolutely this kind of news would crucify my father's political career. You see, he was moving away from diplomacy and looking for a run at the Senate, and our good wholesome family had already appeared in some print ads, testing the waters. 'Let it rest,' I told him, 'and it will die as all rumors eventually do.' 'Rumors don't matter for stupid teenagers, but they do matter for people running for public office!' he exploded. 'And I don't have control of people who spread rumors! Go yell at them!' Now, it seemed, anyone who was innocently looking at me was looking through me. I stayed home and began going to church, sometimes twice a day. Should I confess to my father, admit to the tape, and pray it never showed up, or keep fast to my lie? Back and forth I went, one day this, the next day that, until I was losing my mind, and then my mind was made up for me.

"Out of the blue, I got a call from Leo, a member of Solidarity and Poland's most famous newspaper publisher, a man who had stood side by side with my father through the darkest days and whom my father trusted with his life. I hadn't talked to him for ages. After we chatted for a bit, he told me a copy of the videotape had been sent to one of his editors from an 'unknown' source. He must tell my father, but he wanted to tell me first. 'If you tell him, I will kill myself.' I meant it. 'You will not. If you kill yourself, you will destroy more than your father's career. You will destroy his life and your mother's too.' I told him, 'I can't live here anymore.' He wondered how I would feel about going abroad, to America, or France. He was confident he could secure a spot for me at half a dozen colleges, all excellent schools. That is how I ended up here, or rather, Philadelphia. Almost overnight."

"Did the videotape, I can't help asking, ever show up in public?"

"Leo had formidable forces at his disposal, and he put them to use, I imagine, to keep the video from spreading. But the gossip; no one can stop gossip. It kept popping up like mushrooms, and my parents were worried for years, and it alone was enough; my father stayed away from public office. For cheating him of that chance, I will never forgive myself."

"It's been a while now, obviously. Have you ever thought of moving back to Poland?"

"I was made for America, I realized, weeks after arriving here. Only over time did America become a challenge, not nearly as friendly to me as would be, say, France or the Netherlands, or Hong Kong."

"Not as friendly? How?"

"Well, I brought it up, so a part of me must have wanted you to ask the question. I can trust you at this point, Professor, no?"

"Of course."

She glanced at the sun that was suddenly beating down more intensely than either of us had expected for 11:00 a.m. "Should we move to the shade? Over there."

It almost wasn't worth it for the monster of a blanket, but it was apparent we'd be frying within half an hour.

"This time around we need to get to your writing," I told her after we'd resituated ourselves beneath a tree. I allowed until at least noon to review her dissertation, a draft of which I had on me, full of comments.

"You enjoy my company too much, Professor."

"I have an obligation to you. In respect to your dissertation, but, also, in respect to your career. Profs in your department warned me your approach to work was, let's say, counterproductive to securing a position. I share their worries."

"As my mother used to say, worrying never changed anything."

She'd occasionally rankle me with such homespun dodges of problems, and this was one of those times. From her satchel, she pulled a bottle of sparkling water and two clear plastic cups, and maybe sensing my irritation, said, "In truth, I do worry. I worry I won't find a place where I can teach what I want to teach and will be tossed around from one school to the next." She handed me a cup and poured the water. "But in terms of money, I will end up on two feet, for sure. And look: Now we can kill two birds with one stone."

"What birds are we talking about here?"

"Why the Dutch are more friendly and why money is no worry. The explanation begins with my roommate at Swarthmore, a Michigan girl, blonde and very pretty in an athletic American way, who was there on a scholarship that covered tuition but none of the room and board. Her father worked at a factory that made baseball bats, and so they had little money to spare but whatever they did have was going toward her education. I never met a girl more in love with her parents and what they were doing for her, but their sacrifice was crushing her soul, so much so that she was thinking of dropping out and attending state college back home. She was working twenty hours a week at one of the libraries on campus the first semester, but, starting in the spring, she told me her parents had come into an inheritance and she no longer had to stress out. I was dating here and there, and so was she, but then she got a boyfriend, a thirty-five-year-old lawyer at a large law firm. Two to three nights a week, she'd get fancily dressed and go out late and many times return well after midnight, and sometimes she wouldn't come home at all. I guessed because of his age, she was afraid what our dorm mates would say, because after she'd been dating him for a month or so, I hadn't so much as seen him from a distance. She said he wanted to keep their relationship super private. 'Is he married?' I asked. 'I never asked,' she said. 'Does he wear a ring?' 'Sometimes yes, sometimes no.' Tiring of the game, she said, 'I want to tell you a secret, but you have to promise never to share it with anyone.' 'I am the best secret keeper in the world,' I told her, which I was.

"Just after the last semester ended, she

explained, she was looking for work off campus when she came across an online ad that was recruiting escorts, which she believed, to give a sense of how naïve she was, involved chaperoning visitors, dignitaries, whatever, around Philly. She went for an interview and discovered what was being asked of her and ran out of the room in disgust."

"I imagine."

"She let it go, and life went on as usual, which included the usual series of bad dates, until she started to admit to herself she was always finding problems with whatever boy she was seeing. They never lived up to her expectations, and always, after a month or so, she would drop them, or they would drop her. Probably, she had no real interest in a boyfriend, though she had a big interest in sex, which, when she did get it, was always in a narrow bed in a cramped dorm room. So she told herself, let me try this out, just once, and see where this escort thing goes."

I remained calm, an impartial listener, as best I could, though my mind was racing to connect a hundred different dots.

She continued, "All the clients were vetted by the agency before they set her up with them and in no way would she be required to do anything out of her comfort zone. A car would pick her up from wherever she decided and deliver her back when she was done with her date, as they called it. These men paid the agency upwards of eight hundred dollars for every hour she spent with them, of which she kept half, and no date was less than three hours long, and many if not most included marvelous meals at five-star restaurants and sometimes theater and symphonies and occasionally dance clubs so exclusive and off the beaten track they had no name or gave any indication they existed. But what she found most interesting and even entertaining was how she no longer scrutinized her dates in the same way as she did her real dates. Knowing the terms of engagement freed her to enjoy herself and the person she was with more than she could ever imagine, and so attentive did she prove to these men after an evening together they would give her tips or gift cards, doubling what she expected to take home. The men were of all shapes, colors, and sizes, but she found it was all about their approach toward her, respectful or not, that mattered; that, and, oddly, their scent, which she became almost preternaturally tuned into. In three months she'd only had one date that made her think twice, with a man who, before he took off his pants, unstrapped a gun holster from his calf. He told her she had nothing to worry about, he had a license to carry it, but she refused to spend a minute more in his room and left. The agency refunded him for the time he'd paid, and not another word was spoken about it. All in all, escorting seemed a sensible thing to do for a beautiful and charming girl who had no money, and I asked whether they might hire me."

I didn't know what to feel. I'd never been with a prostitute. The dustiest and sleaziest images blew with typhoon force through my head. "*I'm so sorry for you. There must've been something else you could've done to earn a few bucks*," I wanted to say, but said instead, "So, this is how you financed yourself through school?"

"Yes. At first, I had no idea what this world of escorting, prostitution, whatever you want to call it, was. I've discovered many worlds within this world. There is no story I haven't heard. It is like the world of war, where you have your mercenaries who do it for money and those who join the army because they have no other options in life and some who are enslaved to fight under the threat of death and also those who love to fight for fighting's sake, and those who think of it as a life calling."

"And which were you?"

"I will answer you by saying I was a natural courtesan, not that I became one overnight. No, at first, I was all the actress with my date. A duplicate of myself better describes it; they were with me and not me."

A small chill ran through me. This is how she described the psychological break she experienced on the step of that church as a teenage girl.

"I practiced this doubling to protect myself at first, until, eventually, I realized how natural I was at it, how many personalities were available to me, and what power it provided. Within a year, I commanded fees only the highest priced attorneys charge. What I relished most, almost perversely, if that is the right word, I relished giving men a stage where they could act out their fantasies and dramas. Yes, I would give them what they wanted, and never once did I feel they were strange because if I did, I must say the entirety of the human situation is strange, which it in fact is, but, then again, isn't, since there isn't a human who has known it any other way. There was a Swedish man who wanted me to smash plates and curse and scream in the very tone his mother used, for what reason I never knew; a man who wanted to snuggle and sniff my neck for an hour or two every other week; a man who wanted me to dress like an old-fashioned TWA airline stewardess and serve him cocktails as he read *The New Yorker*; powerful men who wanted to utterly abandon their power and have me take them to the brink of the most abject humiliation. All the strangest aspects of this human situation were on parade, all the weirdness of life on this paradoxical planet. There are a thousand human dramas that play out on the stage, or rather, this three-ring-circus complex of sex, and like a circus, the show repeats over and over from city to city. A drama, yes, a drama staged to elevate what is base and mundane into a ritual guaranteeing everlasting life; so long as we act out the ritual of sex it is impossible we will expire because sex at its basest is the perpetuation and promulgation of ourselves into eternity, a way of catapulting ourselves over the abyss we stand at the mortal edge of. Only when we have conceded death's power over us, only when we pass into the foggy and peaceful atmosphere of nothingness, only then does sex lose its grip over our consciousness."

She paused, shook out her hair, and tacked in a different direction. "How pathetic we look holding onto our selves when in fact our selves are the most ridiculous constructions we have, right? I must be forced to the precipice of the most shattering reality to truly feel the human situation to its core; whenever I feel life is going well or the way I hoped it would, whenever I am good little girl, whenever my lies, in other words, win the day, I am at my most removed from the human situation, and only when I feel the sheer flimsiness of my person, the confetti I am constructed from do I begin to fathom how blessed I am to be held together. Maybe this is the reason I chose a profession, prostitution, what we like to call sex work, that takes me to the edge. Blake's 'the road to excess leads to the palace of wisdom,' no?"

"So, to better experience grace, you chose to put yourself at risk. You're an Antinomian! Wouldn't Catholics consider you a heretic?"

She laughed. "For sure! But life is a risk. I only choose not to be part of the charade that pretends it isn't."

"And because you've experienced grace, you are freed from the laws?"

"Once you acknowledge God and His grace, the force holding this universe together, the mysterious force that keeps humans from falling apart, you recognize that the laws are a weak substitute, made by man so man can claim he is holding it together. Of course, when it all starts to fall apart, we usually turn to God crying for help. We don't say, when disaster strikes, 'God, give us more laws,' or 'better laws.' No, we say, 'God, show me your mercy and grace.'"

"I thought God cooked up the laws."

"This was His way of compromising with His creation for the time being. Jesus made that compromise unnecessary, but humans kept demanding policing, to keep themselves in check, because their faith was, and still is, weak. The laws shutter us from the munificence of creation. Under the law, we only get glimpses of God."

"The same munificent God behind all the destruction?"

"There is destruction, yes. But remember, the lyre, according to Greek legend, was born when Hermes heard the wind playing through the sinews of a dead tortoise. When we witness destruction, which we do, of course, every second of our lives, and is required, in fact, for existence, it is not the same as evil."

"If you're the one being destroyed, it's evil, if you're the one destroying, it's not, I suppose. I don't see it."

"Only God can, ultimately. Don't ask me to explain. But don't also ask me to give words to what I feel, and have experienced, directly and time and time again, that radical otherness whose gravity gives everything its integrity and beauty and form, and is deeply missing from our consciousness today and is what is leading to our decadence and ruin, to a world, again, I can only describe as farce."

Just then, a text sounded on my phone, or, so I thought: She was using a navigation app I used too and had shared with me her location and ETA, still half an hour away, so I waved Zeke over and ordered my third martini. No sooner had he left than, for some reason, I recalled the terror I felt when, out of the blue, I was called into the dean's office. The sheer terror of being found out for my internet caper, losing the respect and credibility I'd worked in the heart of my heart to build, the way a good little boy does for his parents, for twenty years. We met in that beautiful office of hers overlooking the quad. The chair of our department and the deadbeat AD were unexpectedly there too, all three seated in conversation, undoubtedly sharpening their butchering knives in advance. I recalled how I took a seat and looked at our department chair whose suit, I couldn't help thinking, was classic undertaker black, and kept on looking at her until she came up from whatever she was quickly scribbling in her silly and also black notebook, and said, as if surprised to see me there, "Hello!" I didn't say hello back. The dean smiled, and kindly thanked me for coming, and though she didn't alert me in advance that the chair and the assistant dean would be there, she hoped I didn't mind as she believed it important they both be part of the conversation. They were happy I'd come and were open to a discussion about moving forward, because, above and beyond everything else, a sense of openness and civility is what they all sought, confrontation the very last thing, the reason they'd put together what they felt was a generous and, indeed, quite respectable early retirement package. I was wickedly relieved the meeting wasn't about my espionage, sure, but simultaneously I was sucker-punched, even if there was every reason to have seen it coming. Things change, the dean claimed, as I vaguely came to, and sometimes when things change certain adjustments and realignments affecting valuable members of the organization need to be made. Look, I could continue to enjoy all the benefits of a faculty member, library card, health care, dental, vision, etc., without any of the usual burdens, administrative, but also, though she didn't say it, teaching. Unlike my contempt for the assistant dean, and by now my sheer revulsion for the department chair, I had liked the dean, a historian by training, who had openly confessed to me during a long conversation a month earlier that she hoped to soon return to teaching so she might not have to tax herself to death until the midnight hours juggling an almost unimaginable number of balls, not to suggest her half-a-million-dollar-a-year salary wouldn't be missed. But now, back to the point, her jargon, *certain adjustments and re-alignments*, as though I were there for a chiropractic visit, vaporized any of the residual goodwill I might have felt toward her. I laughed sarcastically. It didn't go over well with the assistant dean, who sighed deeply at my sarcasm, available to me at the drop of a hat, admittedly.

The dean slid some papers my way and asked me to take a look at the general outline of that package. I did for a good number of minutes, as her general outline was three pages long, and included, right up front, all sorts of legalese, mostly above my head, but which I soon surmised required me to abandon any kind of litigation and vow to keep my mouth shut in perpetuity on the details of the deal should a deal in fact be struck. All that muzzling was a prelude to their offer, whereby I'd keep my chair along with its salary for the next five years before scaling back to three-fourths that amount for five years, after which I'd enter into early retirement and receive a pension of eighty percent of my salary until I expired, which I had no doubt they prayed should be soon rather than later. With that said, not bad, not bad at all, I thought. What wasn't included in that package, or rather, I'd missed it, now came slithering from out of the bog: As a condition of their offer, they asked that I immediately retire from all current administrative duties, which, obvious to all parties present, should've been put in the singular, because I currently had only one, which wanted to bark so loudly that to keep its mouth shut at this juncture seemed a form of cruelty: "You want me off the rape case." The assistant dean now piped up (beyond scribbling, the chair's reason for being there was, frankly, mysterious), and said other members of the committee felt I hadn't been an active listener during the deliberations, and more than a few of my comments were not framed in a constructive manner, and my questions were perceived as biased, if not predetermined, in favor of the rapist, so that, all told, my presence was hindering consensus building. That we speak in unison about the case was now a pressing matter, as the matter had, as a matter-of-fact, grown into one of national importance, with tremendous and presumably monetary stakes, including, unquestionably, donations from any number of concerned benefactors at issue. As for who on our committee had made these claims against me: My best guess was the Flint girl, though the zoo observer wasn't out of the question. I thanked them for their offer and told them I'd obviously have to give it serious thought, and then they added since the semester was coming to a close, they hoped I'd give it serious thought sooner rather than later, meaning before the spring semester and their annual fundraising campaign began.

As I left that meeting, I was not relieved; I did not think, What a coup it would be to escape arrest and sacking for hacking their server, and milk for a decade a cash cow with a decent set of teats. No, I rather, and rather out of nowhere, wondered, What are you going to do with yourself without this place? What will come of you now? If I'd been sent off with dignity, undoubtedly, I would have wished the school well, think of it as a kind of child I'd help raise, and now must leave so it might go its own way, but under these circumstances the thought it would go its own way, keep living and running, perhaps better than ever, humming, that is, without me, was maddening, as though its smooth whirr would justify their ruthless wrecking of me. I wanted acknowledgment! Of everything I'd done, and contributed, not only to the school, but to the world, or, at least, the world of ideas. Yes, so much of who we are is a matter of patiently planting, like a squirrel who stashes his seeds around the garden. We know winter will come, and we know when it does those seeds will be there for us, safeguarding our egos against hunger, and even death. They wanted to force winter on me and take the seeds along with them. They are our seeds now, they seemed to be telling me. Face it: In no time, you will recede from the minds of everyone, and only a smudge of memory, here and there, like some stain of you, will remain. It was a kind of death. What is death if not the noise of your person efficiently absorbed into the system's hum?

What degradation I felt, so different from what I felt a couple of months before when I triumphantly presented what I believed was one of the best papers of my career, "The Glass Slipper and Other Slippery Things," at the Modern Language Association convention, held that year in San Francisco. Sophia assured me she'd be there, but we'd missed each other for the three days as it dragged on, until, right as I'd stepped away from the podium, she appeared out of nowhere and let me know how marvelously I'd handled the material, with my usual "playfulness and flair." Others were coming up and congratulating me and asking questions, so I turned to them for a bit, while she penned something on a napkin, the very one she now slipped into my hand with a goodbye. Who slips a note into someone's hand anymore when all they have to do is text? I immediately thought. It was an invitation, I discovered a few minutes later, to join her and a friend of hers that evening for cocktails at The Ritz at Half Moon Bay, about forty minutes away. I'd planned to stick around the hotel for drinks and dinner and hopefully bump into students and colleagues, and no doubt get even more and perhaps even higher praise for my paper, and I certainly didn't look forward to the drive, but once I was out of the city and wending along the beautiful coast, how happy I felt to be on my way to cocktails with a student who had become a friend and whose praise for my paper, I realized, meant more to me than the praise of my endowed-chair-seated peers.

When I arrived at the bar, I noticed she was already chatting it up with a breathtakingly gorgeous black woman, about thirty years old, both drinking what looked like Manhattans.

I waved at her as I approached and she rose to greet me and introduced her friend, who given our location had the ironical name of Marina.

"I always forget how beautiful this part of the state is," I said, taking a seat next to Sophia on the couch.

Marina, who was in a large leather chair to the side of us, said, "There are so many beautiful places in California, but this is one of my favorites. We met here, Sophia and me."

"I had arrived two days before I was scheduled to meet a client and was sitting at this bar enjoying a drink when I saw her get out of a taxi at the valet," Sophia said. "She had a stunning figure, and still does, but that evening she was also wearing that sexy gray velvet dress I love so much."

"I'm tellin' you, you can wear it any time, girl."

"I remember too how you went out of sight to check in, but about twenty minutes later, came through the door of the lounge and took a seat at the bar. Her body language made obvious she was trying to keep her presence quiet, which, given how sexily she was dressed, I thought was going to be impossible should any men show up. There were only the two of us just then. I remember you ordered a daiquiri."

"Speaking of which." The waiter had come by. I ordered a gin and tonic, and once he'd left told the girls they'd need to keep an eye out for me since I had quite the drive back.

"You'll be alright," Marina said. "You're in good hands." She reached over and tapped my knee with her hand.

I asked, "Do you see each other often?"

"Three, four times a year, probably," Marina said.

Sophia said, "We try to coordinate our schedules as best we can."

"I live in Santa Cruz now, so this was an easy one."

"But she was in San Francisco when we first met here, and I, of course, was in Los Angeles, studying with you, Professor. Anyway, I started a conversation with her and soon learned she traveled to the hotel for the weekend too. For pleasure or work, I asked. I loved her answer: 'Both, I hope.'"

The girls laughed and clinked glasses.

"And when I asked Sophia, she tells me she's in some kind of life coaching business, there to see a client. Life coaching. First I'd ever heard that one."

"We were sniffing each other out, weren't we?"

"Oh," Marina said, "we already knew."

"There are so many things you pick up, little things. Anyway, before long the charade was over, and we were instant sisters. Part of an underground sisterhood, in fact, that reaches back to the beginnings of recorded history, here adored, worshipped, and there reviled and burnt at the stake, no? Don't worry, I've told Marina you're in on our secret, Professor. 'Since we have the evening to ourselves, then,' I asked her, 'should we spend it together?'"

"Definitely, I said," said Marina.

"Nothing more wonderful than meeting a

complete and beautiful stranger in the most beautiful of settings and enjoying an evening together."

"You're so sweet, girl."

The waiter came back with my drink.

"She was your student?" Marina asked.

"Yes, one of my best, if not, in many ways, my very best, though she wasn't in my department."

"Now, I have to know: What'd you think when she told you she was an escort? Being a professor and all."

"She explained it all to me one afternoon, at a park. I was shocked, honestly."

She nodded her head, sympathetically.

"Or maybe shocked is too strong a word. More like surprised. It brought a lot of parts that were floating in the air and blurry into focus."

"Did she look different to you after that?"

I took a sip of my gin and tonic. The answer was complicated, and before I could formulate it, Marina said, "A lot of people are so judgmental. Way I see it, all they got to do is read the Bible: Genesis says Adam and Eve were naked, and they felt no shame."

I said, "With the career you've both chosen, more than a few, I'd guess, would interpret that verse differently."

"For this simple reason: They don't want to

leave a woman be to do with her body what she pleases. Say it can do this but not that."

Sophia said, "Like we're little girls need to be protected. Women's bodies are their own when they want an abortion, but not when they want to have sex for whatever reason they please, including money? Nobody complains these football stars or boxers or . . . what is that kind of fighting they do in those cages?"

"Mixed martial arts, I think."

"All of these, turning their brains to mush and their bodies to plywood by the time they're forty, for money. While we are toned and well lubricated till we're old ladies."

On the most fantastic roll, they laughed and clinked glasses again.

"Sports is entertainment, but since when is sex not? And what is porn acting? Is that not sex for money? It is, in fact, the most depraved form of sexual relations, as the so-called actors are doing it for money and peculiar fame, emotionless and empty, mostly. No, in America, the ironies are monumental," Sophia said.

"Way I see, though, women use their sex for money all the time. It's nice a man is funny and handsome, but tell a girl lookin' for a ring he works electronics at Walmart and see what she'll do. Tell her he's got a yacht and Rolls and watch her line up and a hundred other girls right behind her."

Sophia said, "Yes. Let's face it, not only is prostitution the oldest profession in the world, but it is also the most commonly practiced."

"May I ask how you got into escorting, Marina."

"I told you he would ask this kind of questions. Professors don't fear to ask questions the way normal people do. Even if they just met you."

"And I don't mind answering, even though I just met him."

I smiled. "Well, if you're up to it, with a near stranger."

"That's a story. A long one."

"I love stories. I'm a literary critic, after all."

"And I'm independent, been since twenty, but I started escorting when I was seventeen, with all sorts of promises from my pimp, Shawnee. He had five girls in his stable, and for the most part, treated us good: clothes and purses and drugs and parties, so long as we delivered. But now and then I'd hook up with girls worked independent, businesswomen, with their own profiles and websites and reviews on the boards and every penny they made went into their pocket. So, when I turned twenty like I said, I decided I wanted to try that for my own. I had a once-a-week regular, a nice guy who was an accountant, and so, to make an excuse, I told Shawnee this guy wanted to be my sugar daddy and I wanted out because he was going to take care of me. 'I set you up on this dick, take care and teach you everything you know, and now you going to jump like you don't owe me nothing! You ain't gonna be nobody's sugar baby,' he told me. 'Well, then, I want out anyway,' I told him back. 'This ain't 'bout no sugar daddy; you lookin' to go rogue. You know shit happens to girls who go there, with nobody lookin' out for 'em?' He tried to sweet talk me and promise me this and that for weeks, until I knew there was no way I was going to make it in El Paso, where I was born and raised, so I decided Oakland, where I heard business was good, Silicon Valley and San Francisco money, and so long as you stayed in line popo didn't harass you too much. What a ride on that Greyhound, half of it with some skinny old cowboy, big belt with a turquoise stone bolo tie and shiny boots, who hopped on in Wilcox, Arizona, I remember, smelling like Ivory soap. Such a gentleman: yes, ma'am, no, ma'am, pardon me, if you would please, ma'am. We went through Arizona and then California together chit-chatting and appreciating about how wild and wide this country was, places I'd never seen, some so beautiful and more beautiful because for the first time in my life it was only me and myself passing through. I was thirty hours on the Greyhound before we got to Oakland, where, first thing, what happened was I was waiting for my luggage from the side of the bus when a big black Mercedes C-Class rolls up across the street. Same whip as my pimp's. I thought I was seeing things, but then I saw him straight out and next to him, Raymond, one of his thugs. He followed me all the way to California? He never smacked any of his girls around, no, he was a sweet talker, but if he'd come that far, I wasn't so sure what he'd do. People were getting in and out of cars with luggage, and then I saw a police car pull up at the back of the loading zone. That's when I walked right up to Shawnee and start cussing him out good, screaming so loud popo looked to know what was up, and seeing trouble, two cops headed my way. Just like I planned. Shawnee got all panicked and took off, real slow. I didn't hold back on popo; I told them I was hoing for this pimp and he'd followed me all the way from El Paso to reclaim my ass, and good chance he'd tail me to wherever I ended up that night and drag me back in the booty of his car. I was shaking from fear, telling them all this, lying through my teeth I was done with that life. The cops asked me if I had anywhere to go. I didn't, and so they gave me the address for a women's shelter. Though they couldn't take me there, they said if I'd take a taxi, they'd follow behind and keep an eye out until I got inside. I've had I don't even know how many clients who were cops. Plenty. I stayed there at that women's shelter for a week and kept my head low. I figured because of the police escort they had to keep some decent distance and probably lost track of me."

"What a story," I said.

Sophia said, "Our two stories so different, no? How you started and how I did."

"Night and day," Marina said. "Night aaand day."

Marina was fingering a small silver cross at her neck. I couldn't help but wonder what her clients would think of it. Did she take it off before opening the door? If she didn't, would it remind, or the opposite, acquit them of their sins? I wondered until the question got the better of me, and by means of fishing for satisfaction, said, "Beautiful cross," which it was.

"Why thank you," she said.

"You know, Professor, Marina played an important part in my return to religion."

Marina said, "The God flame was always there."

"We were in San Diego. We knew each other about a year then, no, Marina?"

"About that."

"He's always wondered how I could be religious, no, Professor?, since it's almost obligatory you be an atheist if you're an academic these days."

Marina said, "Truth, I didn't graduate high school, but when I was a kid, grandma took me to church, hail or rain. Before we went to bed or broke any bread, we always said a prayer. And we had a lot to pray about, believe me."

"Honestly," Sophia said, "not a single one of the atheists I've met much impressed me."

"Really now?"

"You're the exception, Professor. In fact, most atheists, they are as fanatical in their hatred of believers as believers are in their love of God. Except atheists can never recognize the healing power of grace; they work in a closed system, where there is nothing more than an exchange of power, pain, and resentments, a never-ending upping of the other and settling of scores. Only transcendence can deliver people from their bitterness and let them find a window out of themselves, onto anything like peace."

"And surrender," Marina said. "Don't forget that. Surrendering to God."

Sophia smiled and said, "Marina, tell him the story you told me that night."

"That goes back to about three months after I was in the Bay Area," Marina started, into what would prove to be one of the most chilling stories I'd ever heard. "I didn't know what I was doing, posting, moving here to there. One week, I decided to check into a hotel in Concord to see if I could drum up some business, not the best hotel, but the manager of the place was cool with escorts, and it was off the LE radar. I'd put an ad up on Craigslist and had got out of the shower when there was a knock at my door. Figured it was housekeeping, but when I opened the door a hoodlum was standing there, said that if I wanted to work there I had to pay a cut of my action to him since he owned all the girls who worked that hotel and controlled that turf. I laughed and slammed the door. He called me ho and bitch and was throwing around all sorts of insults and I told him to beat it, or else I'd call the manager. Things went okay that evening, and my last client had just left, around 2:00 a.m., when there was a knock at the door. I figured my date had left something behind, but when I opened the door there were two guys, the enforcer, same guy as before, and from all that bling what looked like the pimp he was enforcing for. They shoved their way in and told me sit and they'd splain me how it was going to go down. The action I had that night, they wanted their cut. 'You never done nothin' for me, why I gonna give you shit. Don't nobody but me own my body; and Jesus'—for some reason out of nowhere I told them—'He own my soul.' 'Nobody give shit about yo soul, ho, it's your pussy money we comin' fo. Whatever that pussy done made we want half it.' 'Let me think on it,' I said, to get them out of there. The enforcer said the thinkin' part was over when he first came knockin'. Now was the time to pay, or pay, and all a sudden he pulls out a llama and before I knew it, he was slammin' at my head, whack, whack, whack. I actually heard my own skull crack, split open like a piñata, but somehow I fought hard, kicking and screaming all the way into the bathroom until I guess they figured party was over or they'd banged me up good enough, and left. I don't know how many minutes ticked off, but when I looked in the mirror my face, it was a bloody mask, blood was drip-dripping from the ends of my hair. Even looking at the mess I was, all I needed was to wash up, wash up, slap on some bandages, take some Tylenol, and get to bed. I don't know what my brain was thinking, probably adrenaline."

She now pulled her hair back, turned and

tilted her head to show me a scar running up the back of her ear. "I thought I should call someone to let them know, but when I went to get my phone, they'd stole my purse where I'd put it. All my contacts and regulars were there on that phone. This is when I started to feel dizzy and sick and went outside and sat next to my door so someone could find me if I passed out, what happened, because next thing I'm in an ambulance, sirens blaring. All the way in that ambulance that night, and then, lying there in that hospital bed, that was the worst: All I could think of was how alone I was, how ugly my life had turned out; how what happened to me was, like they say, just a matter of time. My mom was an addict, and my daddy was who knows who, and the only one who ever loved on me regular was my grandma, who was already dead, so that when the nurse asked me if I had someone I could call, I shook my head 'no.' Nobody anyway that would visit me in the hospital, and if there was somebody, I didn't know their number by heart. For some reason, not knowing nobody's phone number by heart broke my heart. The only number I knew was the good Lord's, M-Y-J-E-S-U-S. In fact, Jesus, who I hadn't talked to in quite some time, was still holding onto the line. He never hangs up on you. And so we had our talk right there, with me in the hospital bed."

"Amen," Sophia said.

"In Matthew, 'the hos are goin' to heaven first,' it says. Know why? Because we see it all, to bottom, and know what we're made of. What everybody's made of. Sex puts everything out there; reason people want to act like it don't exist or twist it this way and that so they can control it. What I was to them Concord punks, a body there to drag through the mud, but what they couldn't see was Jesus, that little candle my grandma had lit for me all the way back in Sunday school. This cross, it's a candle, a reminder of the God flame. It never leaves my neck."

"Amazing, Professor, no?"

"Yes."

"We were in a hotel suite in Corona Del Mar, waiting for our clients. Her story grabbed my heart like this," Sophia said, and clenched her fist.

"And right there, at the side of that hotel bed, we said a little prayer."

"Yes, she asked me if I wanted to pray, and so we kneeled there and said the Jesus prayer. Lord Jesus, Son of God, have mercy upon me, a sinner."

"Says it all."

Sophia crossed her heart and then picked up her drink and the two girls toasted, yet again, and turned to matters decidedly less religious: Where they'd recently ventured, comedies they'd watched unfold, and, of course, men who'd called on them, including one of Marina's regulars, a Vegas card shark who was so respectful and decent-natured she admitted to nearly falling in love with him, though his penis was a mere two inches long. "He was all man, but physical-wise, it was like being with another girl, almost." Apropos, Sophia recounted an encounter with a man who was a crossdresser, turning Sophia, for a night, she supposed, into a lesbian.

On and on I listened to their beautiful and taboo-free banter, their dazzling feminine banter, a seemingly endless wave of it coming in from out of nowhere and splashing here and there. I'd asked the girls to keep track of my drinking, but they'd lost track of me as assuredly as I'd lost track of myself. Mercifully lost track of myself, I should add, because around midnight, a good two and a half drinks into the evening, I was dreaming of taking Sophia to bed and suffering whatever the hellish consequences should the inquisitors find out. But just as suddenly as she'd invited me, at 1:00 a.m. she was showing me the door. I assumed she had some life coaching to do.

"It was so good to see you, Professor, and,

again, what a wonderful paper."

"I hope it isn't the last time," Marina said, and, naturally, I said, "I hope it isn't too."

I sat with my martini, parsing parts of that incredible evening until my phone announced an incoming text: "Getting off the freeway. So looking forward to seeing you again."

"Should I have a drink ready for you?"

"Manhattan would be wonderful."

I looked for my waiter, but failing to see him, gestured to the novelist, who came right over.

"Professor. Can I get you something?"

"If you don't mind, Jonathan. My date is coming in a few minutes, and I'd like a Manhattan ready for her when she arrives. Can you let my waiter know?"

"Not a problem."

"Thank you. And, again, I wish you well with your book. It takes guts, and I pray you'll accomplish what you set out to do in spades."

"That means a lot to me. I'll let Zeke know."

Once he was gone, I returned to that evening at Half Moon Bay, for a final recollection: "Should I tell you both about my most unusual date with a client?" Sophia asked us.

"Lips are sealed, girl."

"I'd seen this guy every month for about a year

and a half. He worked on an oil platform off the Channel Islands; an honest, hardworking man, and had scars everywhere, I can tell you, to prove it. His kids were raised and gone off, and though he made unusually good money, he lived, I gathered, in a small house in Ventura and drove a ho-hum car. Sex with me, he said, was one of the only things he looked forward to anymore, hard to believe, but even there, the last two dates fell flat."

"With you, girl?"

"Despite my greatest efforts."

"His head must've been way way off in the yonder. So sad for that beau."

"He had scheduled our date at a posh hotel in Santa Barbara, which he paid for and insisted we spend the evening at. We had a nice dinner, but his smiles were forced and the conversation was all about me, and I noticed he picked at his food like a bird. I could see already it wasn't going to go well for him. Again. I wondered what I could do to help."

"Like a true professional, hun."

Sophia reached over to touch Marina's arm, caressed it, and said, "Back in the room, he wanted to take a quick shower, but when he reached into his valise for his toiletry bag, I saw an unusual flash of metal, what I thought was a whiskey flask, something, anyway, he buried deep before heading for the bathroom. When I heard the shower door shut, I went to see what it was, only to discover a gun, a revolver."

"And you're thinkin', 'what the . . .?'"

"Just looking at a gun, the atmosphere changes, the potential of it. The power of life and death suddenly enters the room, no? I checked, of course, to see if it was loaded, and for bullets in the valise, and found none."

"Hmm. Now, I bet, a different kettle is coming to a boil in your head."

"It would hardly be the first time a gun was brought on stage as a prop in the play."

"Most part, men want to dominate it physical, women emotional. Truth old as Eve."

"Like everything," I said, "I suppose it's a bell curve."

"But for men, the physical curve has all but flatlined, no?"

"What are you thinking of?" I asked.

"How men spend their physical lives moldering at a desk, how blue-collar work is turned over to robots and other intelligent machines. Consider how war is waged at a remove, remotely controlled, and so on."

"Even how sex has become virtual," I added.

'Don't have to change a CD anymore," Marina said.

"All of it inflicts damage in ways we are barely aware of. The growing uselessness of what men were built for," she said. "Anyway, when he came out in a white bathrobe, I was holding the gun. I told him I'd seen it when he went for his toiletry bag, and my safety was, and always would be, more important than his privacy. 'Don't be concerned,' he said, 'I'm sorry if I scared you.' 'They do not scare me, rest assured. I know them inside out. In fact, I once had a lover who was a collector of firearms, and he tutored me on them, and many other matters. But why did you bring it along?' I asked. He was sitting in the corner, and turned his head down and away from me, in what I took to be his embarrassment. I told him I was going to clean the gun, which wasn't very dirty, but, anyhow, I got up to gather from my valise some polish remover, non-acetone, and some cotton swabs and a long eyebrow pencil. He finally answered my question, in a way. 'They are decommissioning the last of the oil rigs I work on.' He then explained he had no idea where he would end up if he would end up anywhere at all."

"Reason he was so sad all along."

"That was the least of his reasons. Soon enough, the floodgates opened, as they say. He told me of one after another hit he'd taken over the past two years: about his pathetic kids, who kept hectoring him for money; about his ex-wife, a heroin addict, whom he still loved even after being divorced for seven years; a lapse of judgment on the job that led to a lawsuit; his black Labrador he'd had to put down. But it wasn't these misfortunes and heartbreaks by themselves, no, what had made getting up in the morning all but impossible, he told me, was the growing illumination of the pointlessness of existence itself; the banality of our hopes and dreams. He'd been on every medication for depression known to man, and now . . ."

"Don't say it, girl."

"He was suicidal."

"But still seeing you regular. Hmm."

"For more than a few men we date, I imagine, we are a refuge, but the refuge of last resort?"

Marina said, "Long as I've been in the game, a suicidal would've been a first for me."

"He apologized for laying his troubles at my feet, and to retire me and the evening went for his wallet he'd left on the side table and began pulling out hundred-dollar bills, until I calmly asked, 'Where are the bullets?' Just as calmly, if not absolutely politely, he said, 'In the front pocket of my jacket. I only keep one.' 'Leave the money be,' I told him. 'We are nowhere near done for the evening.'

The confusion, what to do, what not to do, that filled me as I went to retrieve it was paralyzing, but I kept my composure and stuck the round securely behind my ear, I don't know why, like a pencil. I had him disrobe and lie down on the bed, and then I got on top of him. 'Why did you want to see me again?' I asked. 'I don't know.' 'Of course you know, maybe you don't want to admit it. So, do you want me to be your therapist tonight or your lover? The rate will be the same.'"

"Did you really say that?" I stupidly asked.

"And then I said, 'Well? I would suggest the latter. If you are going to kill yourself, you might as well go out with a bang.'"

Marina put her hand to her mouth.

"All I knew was if I could bring him back to the innocence and goodness of his body, let it know pleasure, joy, I could send his morbid thoughts packing for a while. Nothing like 'the little death' to chase off the big one, no? 'So, tell me,' I asked, 'Does this turn you on?' I put the gun to my head."

To cool herself down, Marina was now using her hand for a fan.

"'No,' he said. 'It doesn't.' 'Well, how about this, then?' I lay on the bed, and put the gun in my mouth."

Sophia sighed, took a sip of her Manhattan,

and Marina, also sighing, followed suit.

As for me? I must confess, this image of all five foot seven of her naked on her back and tempting me to fuck her, with a shiny gun in her mouth, was inexplicably exhilarating.

I came to when Marina asked, "But how about them pretty little teeth?"

"Naturally, with all the inevitable banging and clanging, I didn't want to risk chipping them, so I got a towel and wrapped it around the muzzle."

Marina winced.

"Perhaps it was the ultimate sacrifice, however much staged, I was willing to make of myself that did it, I don't know. So exposed were we both, no?"

She put the question to us, but also, it seemed, to herself, given how long she let it sit, waiting for an answer.

"With each thrust, I felt he was begging for another breath of life, stoking a strange flame in my heart, one that overwhelmed me with emotion, that he would need it so desperately, that everything in me was so shaped to give it to him. To give, to give, for the life and succor of each other is what we are here for, but now to know it as a flame, that flowered until it consumed me, consumed us both, until, at orgasm, we were both reduced to the purest of tears, I tell you. It took me nearly fifteen minutes to catch my breath, to come back from my own, let's say, annihilation, and when I did, I rolled over to find he was still crying, so gently I hadn't heard. 'When you think about suicide, do you think of doing it here?' I said, putting a finger to his forehead, 'or here?' I asked, and pressed the same finger against his heart. He pointed to his head. 'I thought so,' I told him. 'There is a reason men don't blow their hearts out. In fact, they don't blow their brains out; they blow their minds out because that is the source of the torment. Is that right?' He said, 'That's how it feels. When you can't escape it.' 'But you can think of a time when your mind escaped to anywhere it pleased, when it made you smile, brought you peace, no? Your thoughts come and go,' I told him, 'good and evil, the cradle and the cross, day and night, but this'—I now reached for the gun and pressed it to his heart—'this is where the gift, the miracle of life lies. But it is so quiet in its work, we forget it is even there.'"

Marina now tapped on her own heart, nodding in agreement.

"Do you ask it to beat; do you negotiate with it; do you know what great extremes it would take to stop it? Every beat, that tiniest spark, is God demonstrating his grace, announcing his presence in you."

"Why the good book says," Marina said, "body's the temple of God."

"Let's not forget, girls, the heart beats because of an electrical current." I must have reflexively inserted this professorial and artless fact as a damper, if not as a sort of psychic defense against their spiritual sincerity, which was suddenly too naked to bear.

"And what causes that current? The elements. Sodium, calcium, potassium, magnesium, all born in the stars, in their merging, their explosion, their death. And what brought all that into existence?"

"The creator, who else?" Marina said.

"You'll have to forgive me. This is all pretty otherworldly. Did you continue to see him?"

"After that evening, I lost contact. I have no idea, to this day, where he is, if he is with us at all. I like to think his job took him to another city or state. In the deepest part of me I believed, and still do believe, that his desperation and emptiness had been breached, that our lovemaking had healed him, filled him with a certain hope, but, of course, how could I know for sure."

When I looked up from these thoughts, all at once, it seemed that the room was glowing from within: the champagne and vodka, the gin and priceless sake sweating in a huge silver chalice at the bar; the Chinese vases and polished leather chairs and the fireplace loaded with logs mildly crackling; all of it a most exquisite stage to enact our human drama, a stage made all the more beautiful and miraculous for its proximity to the ocean, its intimate dance, even, with the most violent and vanquishing force on our planet. When I reached for my martini glass, alas, there she was, my Sophia, coming through the door. Dressed to kill. Ravishing as ever.

CPSIA information can be obtained
at www.ICGtesting.com
Printed in the USA
FSHW021058170719
60102FS